Just Bart

Just Bart

E.D.E. Bell

Atthis Arts
Detroit, Michigan

Just Bart

Copyright © 2021 by E.D.E. Bell
edebell.com

This is a work of fiction.

Cover and interior design by G.C. Bell and E.D.E. Bell

All rights reserved.

Published by Atthis Arts, LLC
Detroit, Michigan
atthisarts.com

ISBN 978-1-945009-75-4

First Edition: Published April 2021

This book is dedicated to Mom B (Nancy Bell), who read every episode when they were first posted and gave each a friendly like. Thanks for being posse.

Preface

Hello! Thank you for picking up my weird weird western inspired serial, *Just Bart*. I'm going to explain a bit about where this story started and where it ended. If you'd prefer to read it fresh, you might want to come back to this at the end. I thought about putting it there, but this way you have the option. Also, I would then have to debate calling it an Afterface. So we'll stick with this.

First: I've had more fun writing Bart than anything I've done. That's important. But this story became more than that. It's fun, and (hopefully) funny, and also intertwined with depression and loss. Describing it is a bit beyond me. Anyway, here's the story.

When I first started my Patreon account in 2018, I committed to submitting a piece of non-fiction on the 1st of the month, and fiction on the 15th. Being in the middle of the very heavily layered and involved *Diamondsong* writing and editing process, I immediately knew that I wanted the fiction to be freer, less edited, very close to improv. So I started having fun, coming up with ideas.

I can't say what specifically prompted the idea of Bart. I know I was thinking about different ways to write a silly, fun, fiction piece and probably thinking about tropes, and definitely thinking about gender. Very quickly, I do recall, Bart became a solid character in my mind, and the rest flowed fairly easily from there.

After the first episode was published, I had a triggering event (the one I describe in *Diamondsong 06: Freedom*) and fell into several months of hard mental health. Bart and I became friends, and we lifted each other up, Bart finding new worlds and me reconnecting with mine. And we kept going.

At that time, I envisioned each installment to be light, episodic, joyful, playing on old plots with new sensibilities. The mysterious visitor, the spooky mine. Yet with Bart and I now closer, I kept getting pulled by life. Tributes to holidays. Frustration over trying to sell thoughtful writing and editing in *that* era while leaning in on the joys of our art and our community. With those infusions, Bart's story became more layered, it became closer. By late 2019, a bright spot amidst my sadness, overwork, and near burn-out, I was having an absolute blast, laughing to myself as I read each segment back. That stretch I feel particularly awesome about.

And then Spring 2020 happened.

During the first lockdown while watching every opportunity I'd fought and scraped for collapse one by one, I wrote the April episode. It was supposed to be a return to EarthCon, but I couldn't do it. The idea of writing a fun convention scene at that point was not conceivable to me. Just how it was then. Instead I wrote about lockdown, and wrote the pandemic into it; at the time it was all I could do. Its foundation is sadness, but I tried to build on it with hope, humor, and storytelling—the lights that comprise Bart's very soul.

Then, as I discuss in the Preface to *Diamondsong 10: Rise* and hopefully can ease off bringing all this up now, I had a severe mental health collapse, already worn to zero by **layers** of complicated factors and then snapped by another triggering event. When, just after this, it was time to write the May episode, I really didn't know if I could still write at all. I was scared.

Just Bart was on a schedule. I had to do it, at least in my mind, and I wanted to. Through my mental haze and heavy medication, I remembered Bart being a source of joy, along with my Patreon supporters their story was written for. So I wrote May, preceded by a terribly distraught author's note I have decided not to include here, and ended up with a mournful pitch for UBI in a fantasy castle setting, and then for June, I delivered an entire sequence of Bart finally getting fair work from dream-plane cats. So that's what I do on drugs. Yet during that time, Bart was the only thing I was still writing or really almost *doing*, and so to me, those episodes were nothing less than a tether home. By July, I'd started pulling on that tether, started improving, and began working on *Lord's Dome*.

As my fog cleared, I had to consider whether I was going to stick to my plan of 25 episodes. If so, I'd need to wrap up soon, and I still wanted to return to EarthCon. I considered extending the serial to account for the detour, but that didn't feel right. To try and take something that had intertwined with reality enough to try and comfort us through it, and curve it all the way back around to end on a har-har or without a correlating ending didn't work in my mind. Not anymore. It was time to move forward.

So I aimed for an October finale, and month by month, followed an arc that would get me there, even while still writing in improv, and with the intended spirit. I hope that it worked, and that you enjoy it.

My heartfelt thanks go to everyone who made this story possible, both my Patreon subscribers as well as the friends who provided emotional support during some tough times and/or gave this book version a final perusal: Jenn, Val, Minerva, Leda, Rita, Jenn, Maria, and Camille. And to Chris, who keeps the Kansan in every trail, and carries me for a stretch when my canvas boots wear thin. And Gwynn, Vance, and Vera—I hope this makes you smile.

I first read the collected piece now, in 2021. I had to consider how much to edit what was, in traditional senses, an early draft. I didn't want to rescript Bart, or cast them into a more refined format. That's not what this is, symbolically, artistically, *and* personally. One thing I did note were ways our societal pronoun usage has changed since 2018. On that note, and for future readers as well—if any of Bart's desire for people to respect their pronouns with normalcy reads dated, that is one good thing to come out of some hard years. And where it still resonates, I hope Bart is a friend worthy to share that struggle.

Struggle. Thinking more about struggle: our struggle, Bart's struggle, my struggle, that made the decision pretty clear. I decided to give it a scrub and pull a few burrs, but otherwise publish this story in close to its original improvised form: evolving, bumping, and finding its way. I hope you enjoy the journey.

What I learned to love about the improvisational serial format is that it's unexpected. Maybe things go a different way than intended. And that's ok! As I said in that now-deleted author's note from the depths of my own depression and cptsd: *The very best roads will wander sometimes.*

Our twists and turns are part of who we are, as well the posse who helps us through them. I hope you enjoy the story, but more than that, I hope you take that with you.

Now, howdy pardner, and welcome to the world of my forever friend: *Just Bart.*

E.D.E. Bell

31 March 2021

Episodes

For Social, Medical, and General Use

Just Bart: Episode 01

The Posse

"Episode One, in which Bart finds their posse ... "

Bart had been alone for a while. With a road that had wound between law and outlaw, they'd stopped worrying about the past. The way Bart figured, they didn't owe an explanation for any of it. Maybe that was their outlaw side talking. Still, there was an emptiness inside. The feeling one gets when they know there's more out there.

Bart didn't know what was out there. But they could use a drink. They moseyed into the saloon, watchin' just a moment as the doors swung shut behind them, but no one turned to look.

See, Bart wore a brass pin, hammered into a sheriff shape. It wasn't a sheriff's pin, since Bart wasn't a sheriff. It said **they/them** on it, which Bart hoped would avoid a few misunderstandings. It didn't avoid many, to be honest, but they still held out hope. And from a distance, sometimes people thought they were a sheriff. With a sigh, they spun the brown canvas hat from their head and set it on the counter.

"Hey," a voice whispered. "Hey."

Bart glanced around. The bartender was all the way to the other end, and the few patrons here mid-afternoon were anything but chatty.

"Hey, Sheriff."

Bart nearly lost their boots as they saw what it was, rocking back and forth on the wood shelf, trying to get their attention. A bottle of whiskey. At least it looked like whiskey. The label, which looked older than Bart had seen in a bit, had been torn to one side. All they could read was, in an old-timey lettering, **Old**. Old something, they figured. But with the label torn, it was hard to say.

A little face made of black outlines, like they were drawn on with a marker by a cartoonist with a flair for cute, popped above the partial label and bent into a huge smile. "You can see me! You can! Hey, I need your help. I'm almost empty, and then, well you don't want to know what happens then." To Bart, the bottle did look empty, but on further inspection, there might have been a few more drops of brown rolled back against the edge.

"How am I supposed to get someone to fill you?"

"Whatchu want?" the bartender responded, limping Bart's way. The face on the bottle grew into urgently wide eyes, confusing really, since Bart had nothing to do with this, and then popped out of sight.

"I'm fixing for some whiskey," Bart drawled.

The bartender reached for a glass.

"Oh, no," Bart interrupted. "I'll buy a bottle off ya, if you've got it. Wild, er, wild day I've had." It was turning into one, anyway.

This perked the bartender up significantly, who tipped his hat, before tilting his smile. "Well, no problem, there, Sir ... or, er ..."

"Bart," they corrected. "Just Bart."

Bart learned a lesson that day, which was when you ask a 'tender for a bottle of somephin, you best clarify the price range first. And so, Bart handed over about everything they'd earned in the last town, nodding politely at the bartender's vast grin.

"Anything else I can get for ya . . . Bart?"

"Yeah, that empty bottle there. It's got a charm I like. How much for it?"

"Huh?" The bartender looked confused, squinting over at the shelf as he walked over. "Well, what's that piece of junk doing there?" He slid the bottle down the counter, where it slammed into Bart's outstretched hand. "This ain't no trash swap. But . . . if ya want it."

"Oh, yes, it's got character." Bart awkwardly waved the empty bottle around.

To their relief, the bartender shrugged and went to check on a patron down the way.

Not wanting any more questions and part worried the bottle would start talking again—while in their hand which would be too weird—Bart slipped on outside and didn't stop until they were on the outskirts of town, hidden by a wide, sweeping tree. They set both bottles into the dirt in front of them.

At that point, they started to believe they'd imagined the whole thing, as the full bottle of Doc Ridge Reserve seemed just about as animated as the bottle with the ripped-up label. But, they'd spent that much for a drink, might as well give this a go. Wrestling off the top of both bottles, they kept their hands steady, pouring the one into the other.

Almost all of it, anyway. They left a small amount in the pricey bottle, because they weren't putting anything that talked up to their lips.

Relieved the whole thing had been a fancy, they swigged down the rest of the whiskey that they hadn't poured out. It may not have been worth the price, but it did go down smooth.

"Hey!" The worn bottle jumped up into the air and spun around in a most implausible manner. "Thank you!" The corked top zipped through the air and plunked back into place.

Dang. Bart stared. "Oh, well, you're welcome. I'm Bart. Uh, what do I call you?"

"Old." The eyes pointed down to the label as if that was obvious. "Oh, frog hop. I hope you didn't pay full price for that." Old side-eyed the fancy bottle, with its imprinted pattern.

"Want me to put it back?"

Old's face flushed with shock, understanding. "Oh, no! Well, that explains a lot. Not sure the last time I had the good stuff. Again, thank you."

Now wishing they'd held back just a bit more whiskey, they stood to leave. "Well, take care."

"You too!" The bottle danced mid-air again, and Bart started to walk away, figuring now they'd need to find a job, since they'd spent all their coin. And maybe find another drink, to forget the whole dancing bottle thing.

It wasn't long before they realized Old-the-bottle was following. "Yes, um, no need to stay with me. Just glad to help."

Old's face grew thin and wavy. "I can't go with you?"

"Oh, I mean sure, whatever." Bart never liked to hurt feelings.

"Yay!" Old spun around midair again. Bart realized they weren't sure how to refer to their new, well, companion.

"Now, if you take a pronoun . . . "

"If I do what?"

"You know, in terms of how to call you. If you're, fer instance, a she bottle, or—"

Old looked at Bart with recognition. "Aww, thanks, pal. As a bottle, 'it' works fine."

"Oh. Right. Well, I'm off to find some work, and I s'pose you're welcome to join me."

This made it no less surreal when Bart moseyed off, the bottle bouncing around behind them. "Hey," they cautioned. "Don't go breaking, ok?"

Old laughed. "I can't break! Stuck just like this."

"Alright, then." And it was like this they walked on, Bart trying not to be distracted as they peered into each shop or looked for posted signs offering work. They kept glancing around, for the townsfolk would surely notice the bouncing bottle. No one seemed to, and Bart relaxed.

As it were, the small dusty town was average enough for around here, and Bart wouldn't normally notice a neigh. But it was an urgent neigh, the sort that sounded like someone calling out. So Bart went over to check.

A brown horse with one spot stamped as they approached. Bart turned around to see if anyone was near them. No, it was just Bart and Old. And it sure appeared the horse was looking at them. And calling.

"Well, let me guess, now a talking horse?"

The horse said nothing, but Bart had a momentary feeling she, well, they gave a she vibe, was glaring at them.

"You gonna let Horse go?" Old popped around in the air. "Look what they did to her!"

Bart saw that the horse—Old had called her . . . Horse, and she seemed happy with both—was saddled and tied to a post. Now, both Old and Horse stood there, staring at them like there was only one obvious choice. And like they made no sense for not getting to it. Then, to the liberation of Horse.

Soon, Bart and their now two companions were walking down the street together, Horse walking with a peppy gait without the saddle, and Old zipping around her as if the two of them were talking. At this point, Bart wasn't even trying to figure it out.

Horse whinnied. **Town Hall**, the sign read.

"Well, you may be right. That may be a place to get work." Bart looked over at Horse and Old. "You'll, uh—"

"Sure, we'll wait here," Old said with a tip forward. "Don't want to mess up your chances of getting a job."

Bart started to protest, but Old had plastered on a fully cute, innocent smile, and so Bart just gave them both a nod and walked toward the building. What they found, though, was a big 'X' made of wood planks, painted over in a shaky hand.

Don't enter. Mayor at Bank.

An arrow pointed left. Bart eyed the sign suspiciously, then turned left to find the bank. Walking in, a man with shaking hands lifted his fists. Bart could tell which people were dressed to clearly indicate being a man or a woman; in these parts the people were strict about that. And this man looked ready to enact boxing moves he'd seen on the pre-show reel. "Whoa!" Bart said. "I'm just here to see the mayor."

"I'm the mayor." A short woman with gray hair pulled into a soft blue ribbon, stood and walked toward them.

"Hello, then. Name's Bart." They tapped their pin. "I'm in town looking for spare work. But I couldn't help see your town hall is a bit . . . indisposed."

"Yes." The woman didn't look too frightened, and she nodded for the man to lower his arms. "Since my election, no one has been able to enter. Anyone who tries runs out in such fear they can't say what they've seen inside."

"Have you gone in?" Perhaps that was a bit direct, but it seemed an obvious enough question.

"I was talking them into it. Seems the local security think it's their job to keep me safe, not the reverse. I was about to overrule them, but if you're here, maybe you give us a solution. Rita," she called, and a woman looked over from the counter. "Reward bag."

The woman walked forward with a jingling canvas bag, pushing it forward to the mayor. Bart was delighted to see it had a dollar sign painted across it. "For when you're back," the mayor said.

With a tip of their hat, Bart walked back outside. They half expected Horse and Old to rush up for the news, but they appeared to be playing some sort of chase in the back field. Bart sighed, and lodging a boot against the town hall door, wrenched it open.

Now Bart had read a lot of books in their time, so they had too vivid a' thoughts of a dead body or a giant drooling spider. So they were actually a bit relieved to see no blood, no destruction—only a transparent shape, changing and floating, wailing in varied tones. The wailing was a bit loud; Bart covered their ears.

"Hey there," they said. "Who's there?" The howling stopped.

The transparent shape congealed into a wavering blob with a stern face. "Aren't you scared of me?"

"What? Annoyed, yes, a bit. Scared?" Bart put their hands down and shrugged, still glad there were no spiders.

The spirit grew in size and got right in Bart's face, howling again.

"Good whiskey," Bart grumbled. "Stop that."

The shape shrunk.

"Who are you? I'd like to help."

Shrinking again, the spirit morphed into a traditional ghost shape. "You could call me Tom," the ghost finally said.

"Sure. Lemme know if there's a pronoun."

The spirit grew again, bellowing across the hall. *"He!"*

"Oh, fine, then, no need to yell."

The shape shrunk. "You aren't scared?"

"No, I'm not scared. But the new mayor has work to do here, and I'd like some more cash, frankly, and you're in the way of all of it. You don't mind scooting on out, do you? I mean," Bart scratched their head, "if you need something, we can deal with it out there."

A tiny sound, like air from a balloon, wheezed around them, and suddenly Tom was small, a see-through scowl plastered on his face.

"Well, let's go then." Bart walked back out of the door, pleased to see the spirit following without any more howls, until they were both outside. "Now, I need you to stay out of there. Do you promise?"

"Sure," Tom said without inflection.

"Great. Have a nice day."

The spirit didn't answer, and so, several minutes later, Bart walked back to Horse and Old, the bag of coins jingling pleasantly at their side. And Tom was there, just floating in place.

Old continued to zip around, more animated than before. Horse moved forward and nudged at the bag of coins. Was Horse askin' for a cut, why ... Then they saw she was nudging at something sparkly up top. A little clip, pinning the bag shut, like maybe a couple edges had broken and the mayor had repurposed it. It still caught nice in the late-day light. "This?" They were sure Horse nodded.

Bart pulled it from the bag and slid it into Horse's mane. She sure did seem happy about that. Bart cinched the bag shut with its frayed cord.

This was all getting too strange. But, it had been a nice enough day. Bart drank some good whiskey, met interesting beings, and refilled their coins without too much trouble. "It's been lovely to meet you all," they said. "Take care."

Old's face turned to a flat line, and Horse reared. Tom expanded into a wavy shape.

"What? What's the issue?"

Old zipped right in front of Bart, its face again very cute. "Doesn't a sheriff need a posse?"

Bart wasn't sure any of this was real. A bottle, a horse, and a ghost. A need to get more work, but at least a purse of jingling coins. And Bart wasn't even a sheriff. But, in that moment Bart remembered something important. It's really nice to have friends. Even if your friends are sort of strange.

"Sure," Bart said. "You can be my posse. If you want." The others moved into place, Tom to the left, Horse to the right, and Old bopping behind.

"Well, then," Bart said. "It's on to the next town."

Just Bart: Episode 02

A New Sheriff in Town

"In which Bart meets a sheriff, and the town
just ain't big enough for the two of them . . ."

"How are we almost out of coins?" Old asked, peering down into the burlap sack.

"We?" Bart rolled their eyes. They weren't sure when their hard-earned money also belonged to the magic bottle. Especially when half of it had gone to refilling Old.

Every time they turned around, Old was complaining about being low on whiskey again. "If you're made of magic, you'd think you could hold that stuff in," Bart complained.

Old's little cartoon face twisted into pure incredulity. "That's how I *have* magic, Bart. Haven't you studied magic? It's got to come at a cost. Mine's whiskey." It tipped to the side, like it was one big glass hat. Bart did have to chuckle at that.

At least Horse made no claims to their money. Well, Horse didn't make claims to much, really. She walked along, stopping to admire flowers, and sometimes playing games with Old. More than anything, she just seemed to enjoy being in the sunshine. Bart could appreciate that.

And even Tom, the remarkably huffy ghost, had grown on them a bit. Hard not to grow attached to anything after a while, they supposed. Horse usually kept her distance, but

Old didn't mind at all, always following Tom around and making jokes. 'Course, Bart wasn't sure how anyone could dislike Old. Especially if you weren't paying for its whiskey.

But, either way, they'd need to find more work soon. And Bart thought, tilting their hat back to get a sure view, that there was another town on the horizon. Well, best to head toward it. One boot after another, they tromped on—bottle, horse, and ghost in tow.

There wasn't much new to see, just another long dusty road and long stares from inside the windows. The folks probably only saw Bart and Horse, they figured. It seemed as though Old could be seen only when it wanted to be, and though Tom was visible to the eye, as long as he stayed transparent enough, people didn't pay him much mind.

"Well, this looks like another of those traditional towns," Bart mused. "I 'spose we should try the mayor again. Horse, I'll just be inside."

Seeming to understand them just fine, Horse tromped off to a field. With an apologetic bobble, Old floated off behind her.

"Guess it's us," Bart said. They weren't totally comfortable with the idea of Tom trailing along, but as he never really asked permission, Bart had at least gotten used to him. That said, they'd reached a good level of understanding on basic etiquette. Bart stepped up the creaky stairs and into the building.

"Ma'am? Looking for the mayor?"

The woman rose from behind a desk, setting a pair of glasses to the side. "You've found her. Call me Billie."

Bart tipped their hat. "Yes, hello then, Billie. Name's Bart. Just moseyin' through town, wondering if you had any paid work for a capable stranger."

Billie tapped her fingers against her lips while a younger woman, one who resembled her a great deal, walked out to meet them.

"My daughter, Eula," she said, waving a hand Eula's way. "Eula, this is Bart. They're here looking for work."

Bart almost lost their hat in delight that Billie had used their pronoun. Then they noticed Eula had a **she/her** pin on. Not a brass one like Bart's; hers was embroidered. Bart was real excited about this on the inside.

On the outside, they just tipped their hat to Eula as well.

"So you really don't know what's going on here?" Billie asked.

Bart shook their head.

"String of robberies. Big reward out." She motioned back to a row of thick bars, behind which sat a hefty sack with a money symbol on it. "We've got a sheriff in town working on it, but the reward's out for anyone who can crack the case."

"Oh, I'm not a sheriff," Bart said, then realizing they hadn't called Bart a sheriff at all. They shook off a little rattle over it. After all, it was just their pronoun pin, but maybe they'd gotten so used to people mistaking them for a sheriff that, well, anyway, this was fine.

"Eula here, she was the latest victim," Billie continued. "They took our family necklace, passed down from generation to generation."

"So sorry," Bart offered.

"It's alright," Eula said. "Don't care for jewelry. But I was going to sell it to pay for books for school. Mama said that was fine," she added.

Bart couldn't help but turn their gaze to the massive sack of money in the jail cell.

"Oh, that's town money," Eula said. "Couldn't pay for my books with it. But the townsfolk, they're tired of the thefts. Pooled it together. It's yours if you can find the robber. And take care of them!" Their eyes met, awkwardly. "Anyway, my necklace is old and valuable. Laced with sparkly crystals. Pretty hard to miss."

From outside, Bart thought they heard Horse whinny.

"She loves sparkles," a voice said behind her.

Dolly Parton! They'd already forgotten Tom was there. But the others, they didn't react. "Well, Eula, we'll see what we can find. I mean," they hastened to clarify, lest they raise too many questions, "I will."

"Yes, of course Bart," Billie said. "We'd appreciate any help. But, you understand, there's no payment other than the reward. And that's only if they're caught."

"My reward is helping good folk like yourself," Bart said, with a little more lilt to their voice than intended.

Billie raised an eyebrow and Bart cleared their throat, looking off to the side. "Ah, yes, so, uh, where would I find the sheriff? To see what they've learned."

"Sheriff Dana. You'll find her yonder, in the building that says 'Sheriff.'"

"I do 'spose that would be logical," Bart said.

"Big deal sort. From Coppertown. You may find yourself in a bit of competition for that reward, I'll warn you."

"So she's not been here long?"

"No," Eula answered. "Came in for the reward, same as yourself."

Bart nodded, then offered another tip of the hat. And with Tom trailing behind, walked to find this new sheriff.

"Howdy?" Bart offered, rapping at the propped-open door. "Sheriff Dana?"

A solid woman with a hat much taller than Bart's swung around into view. "Yes?"

"Well, hello," Bart said, removing their hat in full this time. "Was thinking maybe we could work to find the robber together. Split the reward, even." The way Bart figured, there was plenty in that sack for both of them, and to fill Old up with the best whiskey even—more than a few times.

Dana smiled. "Oh, no need. I've almost got it, actually." She glanced Bart up and down. "Mercenary type? Hmm. There isn't much here; I'm just stopping through myself. Just got my badge from a place like this myself, a rough little town in the middle of nowhere." She tapped her badge, making a dull *clink* with her nails. "Your best bet is to find a town with better work."

"Do you want to talk through it?" Bart offered.

"No need. Anyway, nice to meet you."

Before Bart knew it, they'd been escorted onto the rickety porch and the door closed behind them.

"There's somephin' I don't care for in there," Bart

muttered, as they and Tom trudged over to where Horse and Old were waiting.

Horse nodded, like she agreed.

"Well, you weren't even there!"

With a harrumph, Horse tossed her head to the side.

Beside them, Tom continued to waver. They expected some sort of remark from him, but he seemed . . . fainter here.

"Are you alright?" Bart went to rest a hand on his shoulder, if the round part near the top of a ghost counted as a shoulder, but as it ran right through, Bart withdrew it, shuddering a little.

"Hey," they thought aloud, trying to meet Tom's eyes. "You could help."

Tom flickered a little. "Me? Someone *wants* me?"

"Sure, Tom, well are you part of the posse or not?"

Old clinked in agreement.

"Well, alright. What do you need?"

"Go float through the office a little. Nothing weird," they clarified with a stern squint, "just let us know what she's up to. She closed that door awful fast. And, hey, I'm not trying to take this from her. It's just something . . . didn't seem right. And . . . Horse agrees. Right, Horse?"

Horse did seem to perk right up.

A brief while later, Tom came floating back. "She pulled a laptop back out of a drawer and slid it into her bag. Then she put the bag behind a chair. Now she's just sitting there, peering through the window. It was boring, so I left." He puffed up a little, his ghostly face coming more into view. "Was that what you wanted?"

"Sure, Tom," Bart sighed. He really didn't have to be so difficult. "Well, if she's just going to sit there, let's at least canvass the town."

With the others keeping them company, Bart walked down each street in the small town, first the main street, and then a few side branches. House after house, people said much of the same. They'd been robbed, but not of the items they would have expected. Small things. Jewelry and baubles and anything with sparkle, but also tools: garden tools, pickaxes, even fencing stakes and bolts.

And everyone Bart talked to was relieved that Sheriff Dana was in town, that they had someone here to fix it. Now, Bart wasn't sure they could trust Sheriff Dana, but they didn't want to place any doubt with the folks. So they bit their lip, at least until they were finally alone with the others. Then they vented a little.

"New sheriff without experience, sitting and glaring in their house, wouldn't accept help ... doesn't seem like someone I'd place my faith in."

"Where's she from?" Old asked.

"Coppertown," Tom answered.

"What?" Bart swung around. "What did you say?"

"She's from Coppertown. That's what Billie said. You know, the mayor." He puffed up a little at that last bit, but Bart ignored it.

"That's not right! Dana told me she was from a rough town in the middle of nowhere. Or something like that. I've been to Coppertown! It's huge. They just put in a High Golf."

"High Golf?" Old repeated.

"Yeah, sure, it's a huge tower and people hit little balls off the top into a net, so it doesn't seem like they're just there drinking. You know, an excuse bar."

"That sounds *great*," Tom sputtered, becoming almost opaque in his excitement.

"Sure, it is. That isn't the point. Dana lied to one of us. Either to me or to Billie. Now, what does that tell you?"

The others stood in silence. Horse tossed her head in annoyance.

"It means she's got something to hide. People lie when there's something to hide."

Horse reared up, sounding a huge neigh.

"You ok?" Bart asked, concerned.

"She's spooked," Old said.

"Why's she spooked?" Bart moved in with an extended hand, offering it to Horse.

"No, not Horse! Dana! Sheriff Dana. Horse says she's spooked, she can tell. I mean, you said she's just sitting in her house, right?"

The idea of being spooked reminded them of their literal ghost. Yet Tom had faded back again after his brief excitement about High Golf.

"Tom, why are you so faded here?"

Tom turned away. "I don't want to talk about it. Honestly, I just want to get out of here." He floated off, pouting, going right through Horse, who practically screamed.

"That's it," Bart whispered. "Tom, you're brilliant. And

you, Horse," they quickly amended. "Old, all of you. What a great posse I have."

For a moment, the four just beamed. Well, at least Bart and Old beamed at each other. Tom and Horse were still turned away and Bart didn't have energy to deal with *all* their fussing.

"I'll be back soon. Wait here?" Old nodded, and Bart trudged off toward the sheriff's office.

"Sheriff Dana," they called. "Sheriff."

The door creaked open, and Dana's face peeked around.

"I've talked to the townsfolk, and I just wanted to let you know, you're right. A sheriff with your credentials is sure to solve the mystery." *Yeah, you'll hit it right off the top.* "Anyway, take care and maybe we'll meet again someday."

Dana straightened up. "Why yes, uh, sure. Take care!" And with no further pleasantries, Bart was on their way back to the others. "This way," they whispered, walking back behind the millinery, behind which the road led out of town.

And there they waited. "Tom, you'll tell us?" Tom nodded, occasionally popping out through the front of the building.

And finally, he waved them forward, and together, they followed at a distance as Dana, bag over her shoulder, walked out the other way, quickly disappearing into the woods.

With Tom in the lead, the others stepped behind. Horse made a bit of noise over the ground cover of the forest, but Bart could sense her happiness to be back with the group, so they hoped Dana wouldn't hear. Besides, if anything, Dana would just see a horse. What could be suspicious about that?

Finally, they came upon a weathered shed, back in a clearing. An old forge rested under a shelter, its top shiny and new as if it had been recently used. Buckets of water, shelves of instruments, and bowls of metal rings sat around.

And the door was open.

"I'm going in," Bart said. And with a tap at the door, Bart called into the opening. "Hello?" Stepping in. "Hello? Sheriff Dana?"

They gasped. Displayed around the walls and across the long countertop were pieces of colorful chainmaille. Rainbow bikinis, finely-linked skirts, and a long display of various bracelets. Right in the middle, hung the most sparkly chainmaille bracelet Bart had ever seen, laced with a wide range of crystals. "Eula's gems," they whispered.

"Get out!" Dana yelled, stepping into the space.

Without warning, Old whipped into Bart's arms. "Tell her I'm a cell phone!" it implored.

"A what?"

"Do it!"

"Hey now," Bart started. "Don't move. I've got my phone here, and I'm ready to call for backup." Hoping it added some effect, they waved Old around. For a moment, Old's little cartoon face appeared on Bart's side of the bottle, eyes glaring. "Well, this was your idea," they whispered.

Dana's laptop sat on the desk. "Dana's Vintage Chainmaille," Tom read. "Ugh, it's all the girly kind. Nothing for sword wounds or anything. Though that bikini is—"

"An Etsy shop!" Bart couldn't believe it. "You're running an Etsy shop."

"Here, here," Dana said. "Don't tell them. Look, it's all been sold anyway; people love this stuff laced with gems. And I can't do anything about it now. This other stuff, it's backstock. Do you know how hard it is to sell a full skirt?"

Bart wasn't so sure. They couldn't see much use for the bikini, but they'd already imagined themself wearing that skirt. Their eyes rested on the bracelets. "That one's not backstock." Bart pointed. "That's from Eula's jewelry."

Dana stepped back. "What are you going to do?"

"You'll transfer everything you've earned to Mayor Billie, along with the sales records. She'll get it to the right folks. And you'll give back that bracelet." Bart pointed. "Or—" Bart thought as quickly as they could, "we'll post your picture on the 'Sodsy Frauds' Folkbook group. See?" Bart waved Old. "We've already got your picture and . . . it's already uploaded. And—" Bart had a sense Dana was getting out of something bad in her life, but they couldn't have folks 'fraid for their sparkle, "you agree you won't do it again. Sell the rest here; buy your own materials. You've got talent. You'll do fine. And . . . if you try it again . . . *posted.*"

Handing Eula's chainmailled gems back over, Dana's voice shook as she agreed to the conditions.

"Well, let's get out of here," Bart said. "You know me, never like to spend too much time in one town."

But Horse wasn't moving.

"She likes the bracelet," Tom explained.

"It's not a bracelet," Old clarified. "An anklet. She does like it, and I think it'd fit her."

Bart sighed. "Horse, come along. I'll see what I can do."

And soon, with the others waiting outside, Bart was back in the Mayor's Hall.

"That's sure it," Eula said, running the heavy item through her hands. "An anklet, huh? And made by a skilled hand, too."

"Eula?" Bart touched their hat. "You mentioned you were going to sell it, well, before. If I … let the town keep their reward money, could I have that bracelet? I'm sure then that part of the reward could go toward your books. Right, Billie?"

Billie thought a moment, then nodded. "That seems fair enough, if Eula is paying the reward herself."

"But this is worth less than your reward," Eula said, her face crinkling.

"If it helps with your school, it's well worth it. Oh, and maybe, um, a little more whiskey?"

"Sure, sure," Billie said. "I'll send word right now. You head to the saloon and they'll take good care of you. But first, one more thing. With Dana gone, maybe you could be our sheriff?"

Bart felt stunned, barely hearing the floorboards creak as they stepped back. For a long moment, they held the idea, imagined it. Then—let it go. "You didn't need a sheriff before. You've got a great mayor. Go ahead, now, and carry on."

Yet Bart felt more than a little wistful as their posse

walked down the dusty street together, with the jingling jewels bouncing happily against Horse's leg, Old full of whiskey, and Tom with a little more color than they'd remembered. "Well, then," they said, realizing after all this, they were still out of coin.

"On to the next town."

Just Bart: Episode 03

Happy Holidays

"In which merriment is shared . . ."

This last stretch of road had been a long one. The posse seemed to be handling it just fine, but Bart was feeling tired. The upside of moving along was finding new adventures and seeing new things, but the downside was sometimes they missed being around other folk.

Not just folk who gave you a job or said mornin' to a passing stranger, but folk who cared about you. Who wanted you to be happy.

Bart didn't have folk right now, but they did have a horse, a bottle, and a ghost. They 'sposed this would need to do.

They felt especially wistful about this the last day or so. By the tickmarks in their notepad, it ought to just about be the holidays. It didn't feel like the holidays, not here on this empty road, where the only snow was the tan dust that coated everything and the only jingle was Horse's jeweled anklet.

That jingle seemed to be slowing, and Bart looked over to see Horse was now several steps behind. "You ok?" they asked.

Horse stopped, peering wistfully at the side of the road. There was a hill there. Bart glanced suspiciously at what seemed to be a soft, green hill with an arc of lush evergreens behind, one they felt sure hadn't been there a moment ago. It was hard, though, to question a horse who couldn't speak in human terms.

"Old? Tom? Do you mind if we stop?"

Old darted over without a response, and the next thing Bart knew, the enchanted bottle was rolling down the gently sloped hill, making a gleeful squealing sound. Bart used to do that when they were a tot, back on the sled hill behind the market. It made them smile.

Tom shrugged, or pinched, they supposed, since the ghost didn't have any arms. It sure looked like a shrug though, so they'd go with that. The ghost hadn't seemed as animated lately. Maybe Bart should have asked if he was well. It didn't seem right to broach it here, in front of the others.

"Happy Holidays," Bart said instead.

"Which ones?" Tom asked.

Bart wasn't sure if he was being sarcastic, but they weren't in the mood for anything funny, so they just answered him and tried to stay positive. "Any you like to celebrate!"

They wondered what the others did celebrate. Scanning their posse, they figured Old was the best to get the discussion started. Old was always cheerful, at least when it was full of whiskey. Its whiskey level now was about three-quarters high, so it should be in excellent, well, spirits.

"Old? What holidays do you celebrate?"

The bottle zipped back into a floating, yet upright position, and its little cartoon mouth formed into view, just over its torn label.

"Repeal!" It shook a little in place, the whiskey somehow

not sloshing inside as it did. Bart was glad for that. Of all the unsettling aspects of traveling with a magic whiskey bottle, Bart appreciated when it kept things easy.

"What's Repeal?" Bart asked politely.

"Oh!" Tom brightened up a bit. "Prohibition Repeal. 5 December. Right, Old?"

Old bobbed. "That's it! That was a rough time in my life, for sure, one I was glad to be through. It's when my label got torn." Old glanced down, its face twisting into a little frown before perking up again. "Someone tried to claim I was medicine. Let's say no one was fooled, and I should have just kept my label. You know, it used to say here that I was barrel aged."

Even without the aid of arms—and Bart had a sudden realization none of their companions had arms—Old managed to point to the section of its glass where the barrel-aged boast had rested.

"I'm sorry," Bart said. "That's sad. No one should have changed your label if you didn't want them to."

"It's fine!" Old wiggled in place. "At least I'm fine. See, that's a thing with people. Sometimes they let things that are sad dampen things that are happy. We all have sad things; the world has sad things. The holidays aren't meant to ignore those. They're meant to celebrate what we *do* have—the entirety of our lives together. Our love. Our," it made a clinking noise, "holiday cheer."

Bart thought that was real nice. They'd been sort of sad, so they wanted to hear more about celebrating the happy even when there was sad. But Tom was talking.

"So what do you do for Repeal?"

"Drink." Old squinted like it was maybe missing something.

Tom chuckled. Bart wasn't sure they'd heard him laugh before. "Valid," Tom said, "but Repeal is on the 5th. What do you do for the rest of the month?"

Old tilted mid-air. "Keep celebrating? Hey, no one needs a specific day to be happy. We can be happy anytime, if we just let ourselves."

Bart wasn't sure about that. Sometimes they had a hard time being happy. But they'd listen to Old's advice. They would—

"Oh!" Old said with a gasp. "Tom, now's the perfect time!" Old and Tom bounced together, reminding Bart of two puppets glued to popsicle sticks. "Horse?"

Horse murmured from where she'd been lounging in the soft grass. She turned to face them.

Old drew near, and suddenly a glittery ribbon appeared in front of it. "Happy Holidays!" It turned back to Bart. "I know what she celebrates, but I've never seen it. Anyway, isn't this pretty? It was Tom's idea, you know."

Tom's ghostly form glowed a little more brightly as Horse nudged the little ribbon with her nose. Staying on the soft hill, she turned over to Bart.

"Ok, ok." Bart rose, picking up the ribbon. They took a moment, shifting Horse's soft mane, trying to find just the right way to tie the ribbon so it would look best against Horse's long, beautiful face.

Horse whinnied in delight as Bart finished tying a

glittery bow, adjusting carefully so the two sides looked right together. "But," they tried to say not so loudly, "you don't have any coins." Bart hoped they hadn't taken the ribbon from somewhere, though they felt certain they wouldn't.

"Oh, we traded it for a drink," Old explained with a nod.

Bart decided not to think about that. They felt bad, though, for, even knowing the holidays were here, they hadn't got anyone a gift. Well, much of their coin had gone directly into filling Old, but they didn't think that counted. And Tom, Bart couldn't imagine what gift they could give him, since he didn't seem able to touch the physical world. And Horse had that nice anklet, but that wasn't a holiday gift, and things you give someone at one time definitely do not count as gifts for another time. Either way, Bart was out of coins. Until the next job.

"Well, I'm really sorry, but I haven't got you anything yet." They held out their hands, then feeling embarrassed, tucked them back in their pockets. Bart *always* made sure their clothes had pockets.

"Bart," Old offered, "you give us a gift every day. You're the reason we're all here. You take care of us. You tell us stories. I mean, coins are nice. But friends are better. I mean, I'd like to call you a friend."

Bart reached out and gave the bottle a hug. Feeling silly, they let it go again. "Of course we're friends. We'll always be, if you'll have me." They scratched an ear. "I'm not perfect, o'course."

"Horse says you don't need to be," Old said, nodding sagely.

"I'd ... I'd like to be friends," Tom whispered beside them.

"Of course, Tom." Bart looked at the ghost wistfully, thinking about what Horse had said. "Friends don't have to be perfect, and they don't always have to agree. They just have to care about each other."

For a moment, Bart thought they saw a spray of glitter fly across the small oasis. Bart wasn't sure who did it, and they raised an eyebrow.

"Well, what about you, Tom?" they asked. "What holidays do you celebrate?"

"I ... I've always celebrated Yuletide, you know, it's a powerful holiday."

Something seemed hesitant in his voice.

"But, well, this is embarrassing."

Horse whinnied in encouragement. Bart hadn't thought of it, but Horse seemed less annoyed by Tom lately.

"Ok." Tom took a breath. Did ghosts have lungs? "I'm more interested in New Year's this season. It seems ... nice. Like a time that we can try something again. A time that we can grow."

The silence was a little awkward, and Bart was trying to think of something encouraging to say. Then, out of nowhere, a swoosh of light and tiny windchimes blew past and the center pine tree behind them was decorated in glitter and tinsel.

"Tinsel!" Bart was too excited by the tinsel to worry about whether Old had made the magic or if someone else had interesting powers as well. They walked up and ran the smooth, soft strands through their fingers.

"It's something Horse and I came up with," Old said. "It's biodegradable!"

"Oh, that's nice." Bart liked that idea. They'd missed tinsel a lot. "Horse, it's beautiful." Horse glowed with happiness, still lounging in the grass. Then Bart realized, no one had asked Horse. "I don't know if you can tell us, but I'd be interested to know what holidays you celebrate." Bart would have thought it insensitive to assume a horse celebrated holidays, but she'd seemed happy when Old brought it up.

Horse leapt to her feet, and suddenly a glowing light appeared in the center of the group. "Mrrrh!" Horse urged, and unsure what they were even doing, Bart stepped through.

The ground disappearing around them, they walked out onto a cloud, and after a quick leap of their heart, realized that it was stable! Stepping forward as Tom and Old appeared to their side, Bart tried to take in the vast amount of color and motion surrounding them.

A host of multi-colored horses jumped, flying really, in long arcs in and through the shimmering clouds. Music was playing in the background—they realized it was Tina Turner—and little bursts of glitter popped in sudden bursts, twinkling down and adding more color to the clouds, which continued to drift by. As they watched, a gleaming table with velvet skirts rose up, filled with huge troughs of vegetable casserole, a giant pepper grinder, and a gleaming silver tray of frosty martinis.

Surrounding the display, a line of naked humans ran out through a door that Bart could not see, all draped in a criss-cross of jingle bells. They started dancing together in synchronization as a huge ramp rose to the side, what looked maybe like skeeball, and—

Suddenly they were back on the patch of grass. Tom's ghosty mouth was wildly agape and even Old's little marker eyes had shrunk to tiny dots. They all sat there a moment, not meeting each other's gazes.

"What about you, Bart?" Old finally muttered. "We haven't heard from you. What do you celebrate?"

"I celebrate my birthday, first of all." They waited, as the others wished them a happy birthday. "And whatever anyone ever tells you, that is a *separate* holiday." No one responded, but then, the dancers had been unexpected.

"I also like the Solstice. I've been on the road a lot these years. But there was a time I had a nice cozy home, and a tree, and—" Things hadn't all worked out back then. "We used to invite friends over for a Solstice meal, and everyone would talk, and laugh— It was nice."

"Is it funny," Tom asked, staring past Bart as if they weren't there, "that we would celebrate the darkest day?"

Bart shook their head. "Nah, it's not funny. It's not the darkest day, just the shortest. And the night is the longest— the most time to enjoy the celebration of light that we set out in anticipation of its arrival. The company of friends. And the promise that every next day will bring more light, if we are there to experience it."

They expected some sort of interruption, but everyone seemed to be listening. And so they explained.

"The Solstice gives us both to celebrate. The richness of

the dark as well as the advent of the light. We need both, I think. A time to reflect that the world continues to turn, and we're all just doing our best to turn with it."

Everyone seemed to be lost in thought. Not realizing how late it had become, Bart watched as the sun set around them, and little dots of light glowed on the conical tree, reflecting tiny beams against the silvery tinsel.

"I'm glad to be here with you," Bart said. Tom nodded, as Horse sighed.

"Old?" Bart wondered at the bottle's silence.

"Hmm," Old sounded sleepy. "I'm low on whiskey again."

"Already?" Bart looked at the bottle, whose little drawn-on face was purely innocent. "Alright. Then we'd best move on. I'll get work tomorrow, and we'll try to make it last longer this time." Bart started to stand.

"Wait," Old said. "I'm ok for now. Can we … can we stay here? Just a little longer?"

"Sure," Bart agreed, settling back down. Old rested on the grass next to them. To their surprise, Horse nestled her head against Bart's leg as Bart reached out to stroke her hair, sure not to disturb her new bow. And Tom, Bart almost couldn't see him, as close as he hovered to the glimmering tree.

"Happy Holidays," Bart whispered, wishing at that moment for nothing at all, except the posse they already had.

Just Bart: Episode 04

A Convention

"Our biggest show yet..."

As they walked down the long, dusty road—well, Bart and Horse walked, and the others floated—Bart pulled a folded piece of paper from their pocket. "We should be close," they said. "Says there's good work in town. Solid rates."

"What kind of work is it?" Old asked, making a full circle around Bart as they walked. Sometimes they wished Old wouldn't do that.

"Construction work. 'Experience needed.'" Bart was pleased at that. They had good experience in construction, from an old internship when Bart had been younger. If the pay was as solid as the flyer bragged, they might be able to save a little and take a break.

Bart really needed a break.

"Says here to gather at the wood-paneled inn," they read from the sheet. "Let me know if you see the one as we find the town." Some towns around here had a stone or brick inn, for the fancier folk. Bart preferred the wood-paneled sorts themself, so they were glad that's where the work was. Maybe they'd even get to stay there a night or two. Sleeping outside was fine enough, especially when the posse conjured a soft patch of grass. But sometimes it was nice to have a room.

As for conjurin', they never knew who was doing it.

Old was made of magic, but there sure seemed to be a lot of things conjured to Horse's liking. And Tom, he was a ghost. Ghosts must have some kinda' magic, or they wouldn't be able to hang around.

The town came into view, punctuated by a tall steeple. "Maybe we can visit a service while we're there."

Old groaned.

"What? I like a service sometimes, if it's the welcoming kind." Bart didn't really have a specific set of beliefs, but once they'd started believing in the magic bottle, they'd become less particular. Who knew what made the world turn, anyway.

Horse neighed to their side, and her hoofprints stopped against the road. Bart stopped too, turning to see what had caught her attention. There, in front of her was a weirdly-glowing rectangle, just about the size of a door. For a moment, Bart thought Horse had made another portal, and they wondered if it was another one of Horse's holidays. But, looking at the tilt to her head, they realized she was as confused as they were.

"Hello!" A voice called from the door. "Are you here to report for work? We're about to close down, please hurry!"

"I don't think that's it," Bart muttered, rubbing the side of their head with one hand and holding the paper with the other. "It said to meet at the inn, not the—"

"Please! Now! We're about to close!"

They walked up to the glowing door, but didn't see anyone. "I think there's some confusion. I'm looking for a con—"

"Yes, this is it," the voice said. "The experience!"

"Yes, I have the experience, but it said to meet at the panel—"

"Yes, this is the panel. Please, it's costing us a fortune with the venue to hold this open, and if we go past the grace period, I'm sorry, but we'll need to take it from your credits."

Bart had no idea what they were talking about, but at the voice's continued insistence they were in the right place, they walked tentatively toward the door.

Zwwwwip.

Scanning around them, the door had disappeared, and they were in a massive hallway filled with bright yellow carpet. Something was printed in a pattern across the floor, but they couldn't read it.

Glancing around, Bart's hat almost blew straight off of their head. A variety of beings walked and bumped past them, muttering in a torrent of conversations. Beings of all sorts of shapes and sizes, all the colors Bart could name, and some they couldn't. One head, two heads, no heads. A dark blue being cartwheeled past, wearing some sort of T-shirt. Well, no, X-shirt.

They turned in place, frantically, relieved at least to see that their posse was right there with them. Tom was faded to their side, Horse whinnied in delight, and Old was spinning in a full 360.

"What is this place?" Bart asked. Before their posse could answer, a small hologram appeared in front of them, featuring a silver sphere with a moving mouth. *Welcome to Pffflyggyp. Please check in at the desk.*

Confused, Bart wandered toward a wide desk. A person was seated there—they sure looked like a person—and they waved them forward. *Slfkvuz, xx-yuk-a—* The person stopped abruptly, smiling as they handed a wand to Bart. "Temporary translator, until we get your badges. Now, name and pronoun, please." Bart could see her own badge said **Oprah. She/her.**

The silver ball appeared again in front of them. *Panel Participants. Please expedite.*

Oprah's smile was a bit forced. "Ah, yes, please tell me if you have a special badge. These are general entry." She put a set of badges aside and reached for a transparent box. "Please, hurry, then. It says you have twenty clicks." She peered at a screen on her arm and grimaced. She looked up, opening her eyes wider.

"Er, Bart. They/them." They tapped their metal pronoun pin.

"Still need a badge," she said. "Loaded with access, panelist payment credit, and translator. Do you have a secondary name? Surname? Planetary rank? Lifestyle clan?" Bart didn't know what that meant, but she'd said to hurry. "No, I'm Bart. Just Bart."

"Next," she said, gesturing toward Horse.

"That's Horse," Bart offered. "She/her."

"She wants the sparkly badge," Old whispered into Bart's ear.

"Yes, can we have one of those over there? With the sparkles and the cord?"

"They're 5000 credits," the woman replied, shuffling

her paperwork. "I can take it from your credits, if you'd like."

"Uh, sure." They figured they must have enough if she'd offered. The woman slipped the sparkly cord over Horse's neck. Horse nudged the badge against the table and something *clicked.*

"If you prefer," the woman said with a shrug.

"And this is Tom, he/him." Bart pointed. The woman just looked confused.

"She can't see me right now," Tom whispered. "It's a different plane here." He seemed sort of uncomfortable about something, but the woman was already pointing at Old.

"No outside concessions are allowed at the—"

"Oh," Bart interrupted. "This isn't a concession, it's Old. It/it. We're friends. Do I er, have credits for its badge too?"

"You do," Oprah said, and she ran her fingers across another badge.

"No chain, please," Old said, and the badge magically transformed into a little sticker over the torn part of its label.

"Are they done?" the voice called from behind. It was the same voice that had called them through the magic door. **George, he/him, All Access**, his badge said. But instead of a human person, well Bart didn't know what he was. He was a pretty lemon color with thick, glittery hair, and his mouth came out of his, well, neck.

"This way," George said. "We're almost out of time."

George muttered some more as they had to weave

through a particularly dense section. "Ramen line," he clarified. To the side of the hall, Bart could see a wide food stand. At first, they couldn't read the sign, but after looking at it a moment, it changed. **Terrestrial Ramen** was emblazoned across the top.

Bart was not thinking there was going to be construction work here. But, they'd paid them credits that they'd already spent on Horse and Old, so they might as well see what the work might be. Maybe it paid well.

As they wound through the corridors, Bart was stunned by the size of the place. It seemed with every turn in the hallway, there was just another hallway. Yet everyone seemed content, at least from the faces they could discern.

For some reason, they were starting to feel sluggish. They hoped the air was fine for people here. But the check-in clerk had seemed well. "This place is huge," they offered, mostly to themself but also trying to make polite conversation with George.

"Yes, yes," George said, his voice perking up. "The larger the better!"

"I guess I'm the best, then," Tom said, suddenly bursting into view. He'd been so thin and quiet Bart had almost forgot he was there. He glowed with light for just a moment, then apologizing, he blinked back out of view. But what did that mean? And why was Horse laughing? At least, the way that a horse could laugh.

"Hurry," George urged, "they're about to start!"

It was then Bart realized what was wrong. Old was dragging too, beside them.

"George, I don't think I can start work until we find Old some whiskey." They weren't sure whether they'd have to explain to George how Old's magic worked; hopefully he'd just trust them.

The yellow being seemed annoyed, but he forced a polite smile. "Yes, well we'll need to hurry. There's a booth there. Luckily there's no line. Since it's *early morning*."

Several heads were affixed to a wide body, wearing an embroidered apron. "Hello," Bart said to one of the heads. "Some whiskey, please; whatever's house." Bart held up their badge.

"You've got 10,000 credits left," the server said. "Use them all?"

"Well, yes. Yes, please." Bart had no idea if that was a lot of credits or not, but they wanted to hurry and not stress out George. A tendril reached out and Old squeaked, its eyes growing wide, as the tendril shaped around it and lowered it under a tap. As the whiskey poured out, Bart looked down at the carpet. Where the text had been unclear before, he could now see what it said. EarthCon.

"EarthCon," they muttered to themself, but no one was listening.

In no time, Old was full not *quite* to the top, and it zipped around. Bart felt a little better, and he hurried back to where George was tapping his, well, fins.

"In here." He glanced down nervously at the screen on his arm.

As Bart was ushered up to a long table on a raised surface, Horse went to stand on the side of the room. Old sat down on the table, along with Bart. Tom seemed to be hiding again; Bart hoped he was alright.

A voice boomed out through the room, over the rows of gathered beings. From the front row, a blue blob of sorts wriggled, a big, human-toned rubber hand waving atop one of the blue appendages.

"Welcome to EarthCon!" the voice called out. "Two Thousand years of pop culture *mania*! We're so glad you've signed up for . . . *The Authentic Experience*. Real Earthlings, Real Answers. Looks like your last panelist just arrived, late, just like an authentic Earthling!"

The room broke into a low laughter, and Bart squinted in distaste.

"Now, why don't you introduce yourself," the announcer said.

"Yes, hello," Bart said. "I'm Bart. I'm just a simple folk, really. I wander with my posse, looking for odd jobs to pay my way and hopefully help a few people out." They looked down the length of the table, but could only see the person next to them, a large man in a purple shirt and a colorful turban. The man nodded politely, and Bart tipped their hat.

"First question, yes, you in the fluidsuit."

A being in a wiggly suit filled with liquid rose. "Yes, Baaaaart. I was wondering if you've ever had a Double-Whooper."

Well, this didn't seem like any of this kid's business. Sure, the years in the wagon corral had been a little exploratory, but—

"It's a burger," Old whispered, from the table in front

of them. It kept its marker face drawn on Bart's side, so the audience couldn't see. "A beef burger."

"Oh. Er, no, I haven't had a Whooper. But if you'd like, I could tell you about—"

"I've had a Triple-Whooper," a voice rang from the other end of the table, and everyone's attention shifted.

Bart sort of thought that'd be the end of it, I mean how much could one talk about a burger. Well, except the falafel they'd had just last week. Bart could have talked about that at least a good thirty seconds.

But thirty seconds passed, and the voice was going on. Now it was something about her childhood, and the audience gasped and chuckled with each new turn in the story. Bart tapped their fingers against the table, but no one seemed to be looking their way. So instead, they spent the time looking out over the audience, noting all the interesting shapes, sizes, colors, and fashions in the crowd. It was a very interesting group here; Bart liked that.

When the announcer finally spoke again, Bart figured it was for the next question.

"And that's all the time we have for this panel. Real quick, then, because I want to make sure we get to all the panelists, does anyone have any parting words?"

A few others at the table said a word or two, but Bart just shook their head.

"Thank you for attending The Authentic Experience! Our panelists will be waiting outside the doors if you'd like any of your officially licensed EarthCon merchandise signed by a *real human!*"

Bart didn't really want to sign anyone's X-shirts. They were only a simple folk, after all. And so, in the bustle of the crowd, Bart slipped through the door and saw George, hustling back to the room, looking at his arm-screen.

"How did it go?"

"Hard to say? Anyway, have I earned my credits now? I'd like to go."

"It's an all-day pass," George said.

Bart looked to the others, and was pretty sure even Horse was shaking her head. "We're just, um, missing actual Earth now. And we're ready to go."

George tapped his arm screen and the door appeared before them. "We'll add you to our list. Next cycle's con will be on—"

Zwwwwip.

Bart hadn't meant to be rude, but the moment they'd slipped through the doorway, it zipped shut, leaving the posse together on the dusty path. Darkness had fallen around them, and the silhouette of the village loomed ahead.

"Well, we missed the call for construction work, looks like. I 'spose we can try in the morning. At the *wood-paneled inn*," they emphasized, glaring back where the door had been.

"I hope it's the same day," Tom said, reappearing beside them. "Have you ever seen space movies? You go away for a few hours and find out your great-grandchildren are your age. Or civilization has died."

"Holy Midnight, Tom, the town is still right there. And

there's no spaceships or ruins. Let's hope, I mean, let's say it was just today. Either way, we'll check in the morning."

Bart faced the ground with a wistful expression, and they were glad to see a little patch of soft grass, this time even with two pillows: one shaped for Bart's head, and another just the size of Old's glass body. "Thanks," they said, still not sure who was doing it and not wanting to pry.

"Good night, Horse. Good night, Tom. Good night, Old," Bart muttered, setting their hat into the grass and rolling up against the soft pillow.

"Bart," a voice said, and they supposed it was Old, "we're going to be alright."

"Thanks," Bart whispered. And they drifted off to sleep.

Just Bart: Episode 05

Ex Folk

"In which Bart encounters a piece of work . . ."

Assuming that the posse hadn't truly been involved in any time-dilation incidents, Bart felt pretty good that the work they'd seen on the flyer would be waiting for them this morning. They smoothed the piece of paper against their hands as they walked aside the dusty road, keeping to the scruff for a bit. Bart just didn't feel like kickin' up dust today.

Things felt strange enough here lately; EarthCon was almost comforting compared to the feelings of being a stranger, travelin' from town to town.

"Which stranger?" Tom asked, spinning back around from where he'd been floating ahead.

"Huh?" Bart hadn't realized they'd been talking out loud. "Oh, no stranger. Just feels like things have been strange lately."

"They're always strange," Old squeaked. "It's just whether you're feeling up to seeing it. Or tryin' not to."

Bart noticed that Old's EarthCon sticker had disappeared, while Horse, trotting along happily while occasionally jumping over small bushes, was still wearing her bejeweled lanyard, the badge swaying to and fro, setting off sharp little sparkles in the dim pre-dawn light. Bart peered over at the lanyard. The colors changed based on the view; they thought that had been called Aurora Borealis once by a queen they'd met at a disco. The shimmery iridescence complemented the ribbon in Horse's hair.

Horse circled back around and raised her muzzle in greeting.

"Hi, Horse. I'm glad we're friends." Bart smiled. As normally happened with Horse, Bart had the sense she was saying so back. Well, that was nice.

Turning back to the view of the town ahead, the light started to glow from the horizon, and the steeple rose into view. It reminded Bart of one of those art videos their mom always liked on Folkbook, where each layer is spray painted on, then the paper is lifted up to reveal a dark skyline. Except, in this case, the paint bled over the edges just a touch, creating a soft outline of the little town whose definition grew with every step.

Bart sometimes forgot how pretty the world could be. It was important to remember that. To the side, Horse nodded sagely, as if it had been her thought in the first place.

Maybe it had.

Together, they walked down the main street, still empty of folk. There was a stone-block inn, right at the center cross-road, but they kept walking to the edge of town, where the wood-paneled inn stood.

It was a nice inn, from the looks of it. Well-kept, with cheery sprigs of dried herbs nestled into pockets and boxes: muted shades of purple, green, and yellow.

They turned around to where the meet-up for work

was likely to be—Bart was used to the way these day-jobs operated—until they stopped like a clap of thunder, almost falling forward like a loose plank. Horse nudged them with her nose.

"No, let's go. We'll find work in the next town. Nice day. Nice mornin'. Plenty-o-time to walk on. Come on, posse. Giddy up, then."

Horse almost pushed Bart over.

"What are you going on about," Old interjected.

Tom was glowing bright now, and he'd zipped ahead. With a spin, he turned back. "I vote with Bart. We don't need to—"

"HOWDY HOWDY HOWDY! Well if it ain't my sexy, beautiful, Bart." A lanky woman approached, a good head taller than Bart themself. Her sleek, brown hair rustled casually in the light breeze, over her stitched jumpsuit and ruffled pink blouse. "Seein' you is a treat prettier than this here sunrise!"

"Hi," Bart mumbled. "Happy wishes. Good mornin'. Now, we were just going."

"Who's this?" Old asked, zipping in a wide circle around both Bart and the woman.

"Stinky toejam! You didn't tell 'm, Bart? I thought maybe you came here just to see me." She shifted one toe back and forth in the dirt. "I'm Angel! Pronoun is she! Bart and I use' to be a couple." She leaned over at Tom. "A steamy couple."

Tom whistled, just as Horse stamped and whinnied.

"Shitters, Angel, come on." Bart did not have to endure this. "Posse, time to ride!"

"Did you really date?" Old's little marker mouth drew to a point. "It wouldn't be nice to lie about something like that."

"No, she's not *lying*." Bart paused. "She?" Angel nodded. "But it's not something people are supposed to talk about."

"I'm not talking about anything," Angel interjected. "I just said it was great. And it was!"

She hadn't said it was great, she'd said it was *steamy*, and that was not alright for passing folk. It was just this sort of thing that had—

"Oh, it's so pretty!" Angel was stroking Horse's mane and poking at her shiny ribbon.

"Tom and I got her that!" Old was bopping about and Tom had grown nice and bright beside it. "For a—well, we'll just call it a particular holiday."

"Oh you must be the *best* friends," Angel said, flashing a big, toothy grin.

Bart glowered.

Just then, the Sheriff, a stout fellow with a real fancy hat, came moseyin' around the inn. "You folk here for the construction work?" They all nodded.

"I'm looking for some help stripping wallpaper in the Sanctuary." He lifted up a satchel, which lumped and bumped like it was full of coins. "It's a great shame of this here town, and we're not so willing to discuss it. Now. The crew can split this at the end of the day. You're together, right?"

"No," Bart answered. "No, I'm just Bart, here." They glanced around. "And Horse and Old and Tom."

"It's alright," Angel said, tipping her hat. "We're friendly. Good terms. We'll do the work together and split it ourselves."

The man shrugged, dragging out two large buckets and a handled wood tray with supplies. "See you by sunset," he said, gesturing off toward the spired Sanctuary.

Bart had hoped this Sanctuary had different rooms, so they could at least go off and work in peace. But the wallpaper was all focused around a main room, with an angled ceiling and four neat rows of benches. Pews, they supposed. Horse at least provided some means of privacy, walking up to stand right in the middle of the aisle. She seemed to be admiring the stained glass which rose up the back wall.

With a sigh, Bart took out a small blade to see if the paper could be pulled off. Thrilled, they caught a loose corner and began to carefully pull up and to the side. With a *rip*, the paper came off and Bart was left with a tiny little strip of rough-edged paper in their hands.

"I think we'll need hot water," Angel said, hands on her hips. "I'll go start the stove."

"We don't need the stove on," Bart replied. "It's hot enough in here."

Horse whinnied, and Tom shook his upper section.

"Well, it's at least ninety out," Bart amended. "The point is, we'll scrape it just fine." They crouched down, angling the blade against the paper. Angel had just started to open her mouth, but luckily Old jumped in.

Old was always there when a folk needed it.

"Is there a particular religion here? Or belief?"

"I don't see any symbols," Tom said, floating around.

Angel stood, bracing a hand against her back. "To me, looks like a nice place. A place of community and meditation. A place where people are safe."

"Well, that's sure nice," Bart murmured, resigning themself to stop worrying and just get peelin'.

Bart tried for a while. First, Angel was telling a story about a cat she'd saved from being stuck in a ditch, and you'd think she was the universe's own hero, the way the others were going on about it. Bart tried to focus.

"Isn't it?"

Hrmm? Bart turned around. Angel and Horse were playing in the center of the room, with one of them singing a song. Old appeared to be dancing, and even Tom was glowing brighter than before. Was Tom *dancing?*

"One of your favorite songs!" Angel chimed. "Don't you remember the time we saw the show, and the fella' that sang it was smoking outside the pavilion in his full costume but with a sour face, and you said he looked like a—"

She stopped. "Well you weren't listening at all."

"I'm a bit busy scraping the paper," Bart retorted. "That's the job." You know, Bart hadn't asked for any of this. They turned back to the wall with renewed fervor.

Not hearing any conversation behind them, Bart relaxed a touch. At least everyone seemed to have gotten back to work.

"We could have been married in a place like this. You know, any types can be married in these parts."

Bart's blade clattered to the floor.

"I thought you said this place was safe," they muttered. Then louder, "There's no need to re-stain a wall that's all worked out." They stopped. Maybe not the best metaphor. They looked over at Old for some help, but it was Tom who floated over.

"A word?" he asked.

Not even sure how well Angel could see their wavering friend, Bart mumbled something vague and stepped outside a moment. The sun hovered hot, overhead.

"See, here's the thing," Tom said. "If you're not interested, you just gotta' tell her. She probably misses you, and you can't let her keep thinking there's some hope."

Bart hesitated. That didn't totally feel right. But it got Bart thinkin'. Angel had been a good pardner, and they'd just not been able to understand each other so well. And a folk can't be waking up every day to a person who isn't trying to understand. Or maybe can't. Maybe they just weren't the right pair of boots.

But ... why was Angel actin' so darn funny, then? Just then Horse walked out to join them.

As she nuzzled their shoulder, Bart ran their hand down the side of her mane. It felt better to have friends who cared, and Bart felt a little calmer. They looked into Horse's eyes. "Why's she bringin' it up, then? It makes me feel weird."

And suddenly Bart understood.

They walked back into the place, stance swingin' and hands in their pockets. Horse clopped along behind.

"Hey, Horse," Angel said, holding up something deep red, with a glow to it. "I saw you lookin' at the pretty window, and it reminded me. I bought this glass bead at an art fair a few stops ago, but I can't figure what to do with it. Would you like it in your mane?"

Horse's face swung back and forth with enough enthusiasm to answer that question. Bart stood by as Angel worked the glass bead onto a strand of Horse's hair, securing it up into place.

"I'd like to be friendly," Bart said. "I think we can do that."

Angel glanced away.

Well, maybe they'd misunderstood after all. "I 'spose we'd better finish the job."

"Sure," Angel said. "That sounds right."

They both stood there, and finally Bart reached back down for the blade. "And if you want to heat that water, it might be fer best."

The water did help loosen the paper, and Bart was happy to see beautiful wood panels emerge from underneath. When Bart had finally pried the last piece off, they ran their hand down a length of the wall, carefully, of course, for they weren't fixing for a splinter.

Angel was standing right there.

"I owe you an apology." She stared at her shoes. "It's been lonely for me, for a while now. I saw you and it threw me somethin'."

Bart could understand that. Time sure had been strange. But they didn't really know how to respond. They couldn't go back to somethin' that was done, just as sure as they couldn't stop the future from rollin' on. Angel probably knew that too.

"I could use a refill," Old said, tilting back and forth in between Bart and Angel.

Bart cleared their throat. "Well, come on, then. Let's go get our money. Maybe ... maybe we can split fillin' Old, I mean, it's been a good friend to us while we were working."

"Alright," Angel answered. "I 'spose that wouldn't be so bad."

"Angel?"

"Yes, Bart?"

"It's good to see you." See, once they thought about it, Bart thought that was a fine enough thing to say.

Just Bart: Episode 06

Boots

"In which Bart needs boots . . ."

"I could use some new boots," Bart said, about halfway between nowhere and nothing, as the sun drew high in the distance.

"One advantage of not having a body," Tom said, sounding chipper.

As much as Bart was used to the ghost's comments, they were also never used to them. Yet, Old chimed in.

"That's true!" Old did a fancier flip than usual, a bit of a figure eight. Bart noticed that the whiskey still didn't slosh as Old flipped around. Bart squinted suspiciously.

"Old, you wouldn't get new boots, even if you could," Tom chided. "I bet you could fix that label right now if you felt like it."

Old's little marker-drawn face drew to a point. "I like just being me," it said, starting to whistle.

See, it was moments like this when a folk could lose their grip. Bart still didn't know how a sealed bottle could whistle on its own, and they weren't going to ask.

Horse clomped along beside them all, not even looking their way.

"Horse, are you alright?"

"She misses Angel," Old tattled. "Horse likes being

around ladyfolk, you know. I mean, she thinks we're all just fine and such, but … well, it was just nice for a while."

Horse puffed a little, still looking the other way.

Bart knew sometimes when a folk was missing someone, it was better not to argue. "I'm sorry, Horse," was all they said.

"What kind 'a boots you gonna get?" Tom asked, floating back around in view.

"Well, my last ones were canvas, but I did hear there was a new form of pineapple leather that's affordable and sturdy."

Tom seemed to glow up a bit at this. "Pineapple? Fruity leather? For *boots?*"

"Yep!" Bart had learned a long time ago it wasn't much worth their time to try and fix people's perceptions about things they found funny. It was better just to walk their own walk, so that's what they did. 'Cept, now, that walk was in a real worn-out pair of canvas boots. "I've got just enough left over from the wallpaper job; I think if we get to the bootmaker, I can afford a right sturdy pair."

Then they'd need some new work soon, they knew. But with Old and Tom in decent spirits, and Horse seeming gloomy, they weren't going to bring that up.

"And you know this is the way to a bootmaker?" Tom peered down the road.

"Yep." *Angel told me* was on the tip of their tongue, but they weren't trying to make Horse sadder about it. But, anyway, she'd come from this way and had told Bart about the place while they were at the bar, refilling Old.

The town did look as she'd said as they approached it. Larger than the last few towns, this one had not just a main street, but several cross streets. A bank, a millinery, well this was right fancy.

Maybe too fancy.

Yet the bootmaker was just where Angel had said he'd be, and Bart felt a little out of place as they stepped up the shiny wooden stairs and through the swinging, saloon-style doors.

The room was empty. Thick padlocks covered the shop's cabinets and displays, and the long, bar-like countertop was cleared off. Only a few tilted mirrors lined the walls, all propped against the floor. Bart walked up and saw just how shoddy their canvas boots had become. Yeah, about time, then. But they didn't know how they were going to buy boots without any boots to be seen.

"Howdy?" Bart's voice echoed through the room. "Anyone here?"

Horse's face stuck in through the swinging door. "Yeah, I'm coming back," Bart said, almost tripping over the front steps for all they were confused.

"Bootmaker's not there," Bart said, wiping off their brow before replacing their hat.

"Oh, no," Tom said, puffing up into a much larger ghosty shape. "Maybe he was kidnapped. Or trapped in a cave. Maybe he was part of a crime ring, and they're holding him for ransom. Or he tried to *stop* the crime ring. We need to search the place for clues. Maybe a footprint. Or a fragment of paper. Or—"

"We could try checking his house first," Old offered, zipping around in front of Tom.

"Maybe there's a clue there," Tom mused.

Horse was already trotting down the street.

"Where's she going?" Bart wondered aloud.

"She says he lives this way," Old said, following quickly behind.

"We can't just go to his house. And how does she always know stuff?"

Tom shrugged and floated off ahead. Grumbling, Bart followed along. They supposed they could make sure there wasn't trouble in town or the man didn't need help. But they weren't looking to bother them, either.

Taking their hat back down into their hand, Bart knocked at the front door. Just in case it wasn't loud enough, Bart knocked one more time. Nope. "He's not here," Bart said, stepping back down onto the street.

"Go away!" a voice called from inside the house.

With a sigh, Bart climbed back up the stairs. "Howdy. Bart here. Was hopin' to buy a pair of boots, but did see that you're closed. I 'spose we wanted to make sure everything was alright."

"I'm never selling boots again," the voice grumbled.

That didn't sound alright.

"My friend says you're the best bootmaker she's ever met." Bart ignored Tom's smirk. Well, Angel *was* their friend. Best everyone get over it. "I just want to make sure you're alright."

"Just go away."

Now, here was a dilemma. One's wishes should be respected, and there was no justness in being pushy. But . . . Bart knew distress when they heard it. Maybe Tom had a point. Maybe this bootmaker was in trouble. Bart figured they'd try one more time.

"Are you ok?"

"Yes, I'm fine. I promise. Just not in a mood for sellin' boots! Now, go!"

Bart was a gentlefolk, and the man had asked them to go.

Wandering back out toward a park, Bart sat for a while. Sometimes, a folk can sit and sit and the ideas just don't come to ya. Tired of not being helpful, at least they figured they could go fill Old. Old never appreciated getting low.

Horse went off to play in a field, and Tom offered to stay with her. Bart nodded them a quick "see you soon" and went with Old to find it some whiskey.

The saloon wasn't too far past. Bart wondered if they should mention the bootmaker to the other patrons for some ideas, but it was a moot point, as the bar was pret'near empty.

"It *is* only noon," the bartender said, tucking a cloth into her shirt.

Without much to say to that, Bart slid a set of coins out. As Old didn't like to show it was magic in front of strangers, Bart held their friend out, like a normal bottle, and handed it to the 'tender. "Fill it up, please."

The bartender gazed at the coins a long moment before sweeping them into her apron. "I could fix you up with anything 'cept the top shelf with that. Don't need that old bottle."

"It's my friend," Bart murmured, completely distracted by remembering the sadness in the bootmaker's voice. Yet, sometimes a show just didn't have the right ticket. Maybe after Old was set, Bart had best be movin' on.

Soon Old was full again, and the bartender had taken to washing out a pair of large jugs in the washbasin. Bart ignored her.

They stared off at the wall, until getting distracted by a tiny tapping noise. Glancing over, they saw Old was clicking away at a cellphone—not that they knew how, since it didn't have fingers. Yet, that wasn't Bart's main concern.

"Old! She'll be able to see you." Bart didn't mind if Old showed itself, but Old always seemed funny on the idea.

"It's fine," Old said. "Trust me, she can't see me. Got a friend of her own in her pocket."

Huh? Bart cut a quick glance, and did notice the bartender had taken a quick swig of something. To each their own, they supposed. "Fine. Whatcha' looking for?"

Old swung the phone around, revealing a tweet with a big, colorful picture. Bart gasped.

Rushing out of the saloon, Bart ran toward the bootmaker's house. They heard a clomping of hooves to the side, and realized the whole posse had joined them. Old was hovering around Horse's front region, and they seemed to be talking. Well, Bart had things to do.

Bart didn't bother to knock, but called up to the window. "Mr. Bootmaker? I'm so sorry that happened," Bart said. "I saw the tweets. I just want you to know that I know how toxic that there internet can be, and if you want to talk about it, I'm here."

Not hearing an answer, Bart decided they'd done their best. They turned back again to the street. Then the door creaked open behind them.

"Look," the bootmaker said, his bare feet dirty against the worn wood floor. "I appreciate your kindness. But I'm staying here, and I'm never making boots again."

Bart actually understood. "I know it can feel that way sometimes, when you're just doing your best to make things people will enjoy and people are out there just looking to be mean." Bart almost didn't ask the next part, but if they were going to try and comfort the man, they'd best know what they were dealing with. "But, er, who is Billy McFilly?"

"The *Whooper?*" he spat back with incredulity.

"Look," Bart said, feeling frustrated again, "everyone keeps mentioning this whooper to me, but I don't eat that sort of thing. I'm just a simple folk, who enjoys my burgers beany."

Tom snorted behind them, and Bart threw back a glare.

"Billy McFilly is a *clown,*" the bootmaker said. "They represent that burger joint." He pointed down the road. "Appeals to kids."

Bart remembered the image on Old's phone with alarm.

"I made myself the best pair of boots I ever had," he continued. "Sleek, red, pineapple leather. Legs for days! But there were storm clouds out yonder, so just in case, I threw on my old rain jacket, just for walking across town. Some kids photographed me, an' said the yellow coat and red boots looked like McFilly! Me. Purveyor of fashion. I can't be seen again. That's it. I'm done."

He turned to the side, folding his arms over.

"The world's full of bullies," Bart said. "I know. I've been hurt by some myself. People will say anything to justify bullying these days. Nothing makes it right."

"Well that's nice. But I'm done."

See, this was the thing about being simple folk. Sometimes they didn't know just what to say.

Horse nudged their arm.

"She has an idea," Old said, nodding. "Here." And it whispered into Bart's ear.

Bart wasn't always sure about Horse's ideas, but well, anything was worth cheering this fellow up.

"You know, red boots are the best," Bart began. "Superman . . . wore them."

The bootmaker's head rose, just a little, and Horse nodded encouragingly.

"And, Wonder Woman too. And Spiderman. And, er . . ." They stumbled around. "Boots the Monkey!"

"What?" He threw his face back into his hands.

"No, strike that one. Er, Pinocchio!" Dang, this wasn't going well. They looked at Horse in desperation. "Alright, wait—"

Horse stamped.

"Ginger Spice wore red boots. And RuPaul! And Madonna—remember the sizzling red boots in her geisha look?"

"The cultural appropriateness of that has been questioned," the bootmaker sniffed.

"We're fixin' like we're in a fake Old West!" Bart said. "I believe our perspective is clear! Now, you watch that video and tell me that was not one stunning, iconic, cinematic piece of candy. And the remixes. Donna and Niki! The single photography. Surely underrated, in context." Bart had to stop and take a breath.

"That sugar was sweet," Tom agreed.

The bootmaker still didn't look sure. But Bart didn't have space to start unpacking all the Gaultier, and—

"Sailor Moon," Old said, floating around to the front. "Sailor Moon!"

The bootmaker looked up, his eyes wide.

"Sailor Moon has red boots?"

"She does," Bart said, breathing back out. "She sure does."

Slowly, the bootmaker rose. "A minute," he said.

And when he walked back out, he was wearing tight black shorts and ... the brightest, most shiny thigh-high red boots Bart had ever seen. He slung on a worn brown jacket over his tee.

"Don't say anything," Old whispered. "I'll be runnin' low with much more of this."

In silence, they walked—and the bootmaker strutted—back to the boot shop. And after he'd fitted Bart for the nicest, most comfortable, chunky black pineapple leather boots, he looked up, with a gleam in his eyes.

"No charge," he said.

"I can't," Bart said. "Artists deserve to be paid, and this is ... beauty." Bart pushed the coins across the counter.

"Well, I'd love to repay you for your kindness. Is there anything I can do?"

From outside, Horse whinnied.

And by the time they'd left the town saloon at what was now a proper hour, Horse's hooves were covered in shiny little gold skirts, each fastened at the ankle with a large safety snap and a petite metallic dangle of fringe.

"You look nice, Horse," Tom conceded. And somehow, Horse's nose didn't even waft through the little ghost, but managed to bump him. Old laughed, and Tom laughed with it.

And Bart, who'd remembered to put band-aids on their heels, since the boots *were* new after all, walked comfortably down the street, 'membering, as always, that they sure were lucky to have friends.

"I'll never be the same," they murmured, happy just to be walkin' on to the next town.

Just Bart: Episode 07

The Tower of La'ni'thala

"In which a new, glittery path emerges . . ."

Bart's coins were low again, but that bootmaker had started to get a little more friendly with Bart than they'd prefer, so they'd gotten back on their way. See, it's not that Bart wasn't friendly or the man wasn't nice, but Bart was just simple folk, for now just tryna' stay out of trouble. And they needed some time on their own.

Sure, they had Horse an' Old an' Tom. That was different. That was posse.

They were quiet today, the lot of them. Horse's clopping along was the only real sound, with the slight tinkle of her hoof covers and jeweled anklet. The clopping stopped.

Horse stood, her tail swooshing, pointing down a side path that wound up and around a hill.

Now, Bart was sure there hadn't been a path there a moment ago. And it wasn't just another dusty path, like the sort that would lead to a smoldering campsite looking out over the sunset for a weary traveler.

It was a bit like that yellow brick road from the story, 'cept instead of yellow, the brown hill slowly turned into green, clover, tiny flowers, and glitter.

Bart peered suspiciously at Horse. "Now, the last time

we walked through some magic door I got pulled into a seriously undermoderated panel."

"No moderators live that way," Tom said, the ghost suddenly popping into view. "Trust me."

Old's little eyebrows had formed—sometimes they were there and other times not—and were raised in surprise. "Bart," it finally said. "There is not going to be a glittery path in front of us and we just pass right by."

Bart sighed. Well, maybe there'd be work this way. Bart could use some coin.

They started up the hill, and while at first the path was green and glitter laced just on its own, soon the little flowers turned into wispy reeds, and then swaying saplings. Soon, the posse walked through a full-fledged magic forest, with chirping birds and rustling leaves.

"Is this right?" Bart wondered aloud. "Never mind," they muttered, seeing that Horse confidently strode on ahead, now weaving through the forest as if she knew exactly where she were going.

Then she paused. Her head rose up as the filtered light of the forest caught the shimmering ribbon bow and bead accent in her hair. She whinnied out, as if calling a name.

A double door on front of a tall structure creaked open, and Horse walked forward.

"Horse, I don't mean this for lack of sensitivity, but I don't think you can go into a tower." There'd be a spiral staircase or something such, and even with Horse's unpredictable abilities they didn't want her to be disappointed.

Horse walked on in anyway. With a glance to Bart, Tom shrugged.

"Better follow," Old said. "I mean, she'll be fine, but you won't see me missing this!" Old zipped ahead, Tom behind. With a sigh, Bart walked up and in through the wide doorway.

They squinted in, hesitantly, as the majority of the room was painted with a wide gold circle. Horse stood in the middle, and Tom hovered near. Old was jumping, as much as a floating bottle jumps, up and down to one side.

"Better get on," Old said. "Don't be that warrior that has to get leaped. You know, like in WoW."

Huh? Bart stopped cold. *World of Warcraft?* Did Old play WoW? How could a bottle play—

The elevator rose, leaving a small indent in the floor. Bart heard a noise like a train, as the others disappeared from sight.

"Well, for all the injustice," Bart said. They couldn't just stand there, so they walked back and forth until the gold circle finally lowered back to the ground. And Bart didn't play a warrior; they were a very nice resto druid. Muttering, Bart walked onto the platform and eventually it rose to the top.

Fortunately, the others were waiting. "Do you play WoW, Old?" Bart had been curious.

"Me? I'm a bottle! You can call me the patron saint. Horse plays all the time."

"Horse, really? Maybe we can group up sometime? For the Alliance!"

Horse stood with an awkward look on her face. She glanced around the room. Well, they supposed they were in the midst of a magical tower and probably didn't need to be talkin' about Azeroth.

"And me. I play Death Knight on her server," Tom said. "We *own* Dazaralor chat."

WHO GOES HITHER, a voice bellowed.

Bart glanced around.

Horse whinnied, sounding excited.

NO. I'M NOT SPEAKING HORSE THIS TIME. I'M A WIZARD.

Horse stamped.

The next words were elderly in tone, rather gentle. "Oh, fine. I'll speak in my real voice, but you turn that on."

Grumbling, Horse nodded, and the wizard—they figured this was a wizard, with that old gray robe and all—walked in and tapped Horse's EarthCon badge. It beeped.

"Hey, MageBoss." The human-like words came out of Horse's mouth, sort of gravelly like, well, a . . . folk at a party would sound imitating a horse? Bart almost fell over.

"Haven't seen you online lately, so we wanted to stop in and see how you were doing."

We?

Bart was getting real confused. Horse was talking? Were they visiting an actual, you know, wizard? Or was this one of Horse's gaming buddies?

"Both," Old whispered in their ear. "Per's legit, for sure."

Per? Bart leaned in and noticed a stitched patch on the wizard's chest. **Per / Per**, it said. Well, good, per was a real wizard after all. For a moment there, Bart thought they'd transported to the folk's Garrison or something. Bart still used theirs; it was a place to get away from the bustle of Stormwind. Besides, they'd paid a lot for that auction bot.

"Well, hello, MageBoss. Is, uh, that what we call you?"

"Sure! Welcome to the TOWER OF LA'NI'THALA." Horse's eyes narrowed and MageBoss lowered per voice. "Nice to meet you. Horse, who are your friends?"

"Well, you know BustThisDK, of course," Horse answered. "Goes by Tom here. And this is Bart. They rescued me from some asshole who tried to take me as their own personal go cart, and this is Old. Nice bottle; part of the Bart package."

Now, Horse speaking like a person was one thing, but with a fresh mouth included! And Old was its own entity; Horse knew that well as anyone.

"I'd say everyone take a seat, but we all know Horse prefers to stand."

Horse nearly guffawed.

"So, uh, MageBoss, you're a wizard?" Bart noted the gold-trimmed room, full of hanging glass planets and strange mirrors. They figured it did look right wizardy.

"Indeed. I'm on a council that keeps tabs on dark magic throughout the fake Old West. We try to keep folk safe as best we can."

"And, on Warcraft, what do you play?"

Everyone just stared at Bart, like they'd said something ridiculous. That wasn't fair! No one ought to be pre-judged based on their looks or their—

"I play a mage."

Feelin' stubborn, Bart set their hands on their hips. "Well, surely. But of course I was referring to your spec."

"Oh, arcane. But anyway, we aren't here to talk about that."

"We actually are, MageBoss," Horse corrected. "At least, enough for me to check that you're alright."

"I've just been ... stressed out." MageBoss turned to gaze out of a long, midnight blue stained-glass window, inset with yellow stars.

Bart didn't know the wizard at all, but hearing anyone was too stressed to have fun always got them worried. All people deserved time to relax. Yet, not knowing per, they weren't sure how to ask what was going on.

"Too many hours working? Is Gandalf mad at you again?" Horse asked.

"No, he's fine," MageBoss said, pointing over to where a gray cat lay sprawled on his back. "Work's fine. It's my dice set."

Horse's voice, while still wobbling like a faux horse voice—which had been irritating Bart more than they cared to admit until they considered that the option was MageBoss speaking horse—was kind and patient. "Did you lose them?"

"No, not *my* dice set." Per patted per robes. "My Kickstarter. Thought for sure I could raise the full amount by letting people know what I was doing. I mean, it's art."

"Ooh," Horse sympathized. "The wizard fire dice? You finally got that to work?"

"Yeah, but I've got a day left and I'm at forty percent." MageBoss hung per head. "I've tried everything. Link shares, paid ads—I even got ImSteve to send out a post."

Horse seemed to be in thought.

Old spun around next to her. "Can we see the campaign? Maybe we can help."

"Sure." MageBoss flicked a wand up and a campaign screen appeared over a gold brick wall.

Wizard Fired Dice – Dice made by a real mage, Goal: 45ᴇ Wizard Coins (Approx $4800.00 ᴜsᴅ)

Horse seemed sort of stunned. Her hair swooshed back and forth a little, the light glinting off of the red bead.

"She probably thought it was a higher goal," Old whispered into Bart's ear. "Last tabletop Horse worked on did 340ᴋ."

Bart wasn't even going to ask what that meant. But they saw there was a chunky arrow over the main image and got curious. "Hit play?" they suggested.

MageBoss flicked per hand. A second image of MageBoss, still in the gray robes and sitting on a couch looking downward, appeared on the wall.

"Hi. I'm the infamous MageBoss. You may remember how I tore it up in Molten Core. I've learned how to make dice. Real wizard dice. Here's an example." Per held up per hand and Bart tried to make out something dark in per palm. "These dice are really special to me because I've spent a lot of time refining them. They reflect my spirit. And I need funds to be able to buy the dwarf-forged elven powder used to generate the amount of wizard fire needed to give the right sparkle to each one. Magic is not easy, and I've been a trained mage since most of you were bottles of red wine. I've—"

The video clicked off.

"Hey, there's still five minutes," MageBoss protested.

"I saw," Horse said. "Look, let's cut to it. I'll make you a video. The deal is, I make it, you upload it. No questions."

"I'm not sure I want to—"

"Then say no," Horse interrupted.

"Fine," MageBoss grumbled.

"Ok, on the count of three, you start recording. One . . . two . . ."

The wizard's tower disappeared from around them and, like in Horse's holiday dream, Bart, Tom, MageBoss, and Old were left standing on one little cloud. A solid cloud, sort of. Either way, they weren't sinking. Horse was suspended in mid-air, with no ground at all, but in front of a huge rainbow. Her gold hoofcaps sparkled, and her hair wafted in a non-existent breeze. She began to gallop down the rainbow.

"Think you have the best dice? Were yours conjured by a *wizard*? Now, watch this!"

Bart hoped to all hope it was not the dancers again. Bart wasn't ready for—

About five hundred anime-style otters, colored with thick lines and bright yellow tones, popped into the sky surrounding Horse. They began to sing in chorus: "Wizard Dice! Wizard Dice! You otter get your Wizard Dice!"

Bright lights flashed and something exploded and there was a fizzing sound and Bart had no idea what was going on but they were back in the golden tower room, and the image on the brick wall changed from a picture of MageBoss to the image of Horse.

"Look," Tom whispered.

Sure enough, the little number started to climb. Three κ, Four κ, Seven κ— MageBoss stood to the side, tearing up at the sight. "Thanks, Horse. I'll take it. Now that I don't have to worry about funding, I'll be back on for raid tonight."

Now, see, Bart was a simple folk and didn't remember Horse "raiding" as she laid herself down on the vast plains of the land for a long sleep, but they just weren't about to question it.

MageBoss left a moment, returning with a crystal tray of three little crystal shot glasses. Whatever it was, Bart was ready. They took one and shot it back, almost choking a little as they watched MageBoss tip one down Horse's throat.

"I don't drink," Tom clarified to Bart. "Past issues."

"Well, thanks again, friends." MageBoss set down the tray. "We'll wreck shit tonight like Darnassus." Per laughed, a big bellowing laugh.

Bart's head snapped around, the little shot glass almost crushing in their fingers. "Now don't you talk about Darnassus!" Bart thought their cap would blow right off for all the—

"Settle down, Bart, it's an imaginary world."

"I will not settle down about Darnassus."

"They're fine, Horse," MageBoss said, taking the shot glass away from them just the same. With a tight grin, per walked into the back of the room.

Soon, per returned, levitating a golden decanter with a gleaming amber liquid inside. With a tap of per wand, Old was full again.

"And, here," per said, holding out a small, bulging sack made of some kind of velour. "It's a consulting fee for the Kickstarter help. It's the least I can do. Plus I'll send you a set of the dice. *Each*," per added.

Horse nodded. "Give it to Bart. They'll do good with it. They're just folk."

Bart smiled, pulling the pouch through their belt and tying its drawstring together.

"But, I need to do something for you, Horse," per continued. "You saved me."

Old floated over and whispered in MageBoss' ear.

"Ah," per said. "True. Horse, could I conjure you a sprite?"

Horse breathed excitedly and with a wave of MageBoss' hand, a tiny little sprite appeared, made of all shimmer and tinkle.

"Is that a . . . living being?" Bart was worried.

"No!" per exclaimed. "What sort of creep do you think I am? It's conjured. A bauble."

"Thank you," Horse said, watching the sprite with glee. "I love her! Now, that's enough of this man-speak. Rrrreaaaaarrr."

With a nod, MageBoss reached forward and tapped the button on Horse's badge. The glittering lanyard swayed back and forth and the sprite darted through it with a little backflip. Horse whinnied.

Together, they piled onto the large, circular elevator, and Bart tried not to think whether Old and Tom, both floating, were ascending and descending with it, or just pretending to.

Bart hadn't found work that day, but they had a small set of coins, Old was full, and they'd been able to help a friend.

It was time to make like bear form and rest.

Just Bart: Episode 08

BnB

"In which Bart meets the 47982s
and then we forget this happened . . . "

Bart peered down into the small sack of coins, which in better lighting had been revealed to be a scuffed-up dice bag, with **MageBoss** written in marker inside. It was about empty.

Having coins had been nice for a few days, being able to buy some seitan tacos and even a fresh dish of guacamole and sit in a park without feeling worried.

But those coins were almost gone, and Bart hadn't found any more work. There was a larger town this way, people said, and while Bart was simple folk and liked to stick to the back roads, it might be time to head to the city for a touch.

Bart couldn't stop glancing at the twinkling little sprite, which popped in and out around Horse, sometimes disappearing entirely. Horse had called the little sprite "she" before Horse's translator had been bumped off, and Bart knew Horse was real considerate about issues of identity.

Yet, who was the little "she?" Was she a real creature? If so, she must be staying by choice?

"If you don't mind me asking, is the sprite alive? Or, I suppose I mean, sentient?"

Now, Bart didn't think a horse could roll their eyes, but somehow Horse managed to roll hers.

"That's too limiting a question," Old said, suddenly floating in front of Bart's face.

"It is not a limiting question," Bart huffed, "it's a very important question. If the sprite is a sentient being, then she has rights and we need to check if she's alright. I mean, is she part of the posse?"

"Is there a membership fee now, Bart?" Old asked, a sarcastic twitch to its face. "It's just more complicated than you're making it. Maybe Horse will explain more later. For now, let's just establish that her name is too complicated to say in people-speak, but since you can't neigh, you can call her Twinkle. She's fine with that."

The sprite was making decisions? This sounded real sentient to Bart. More questions would be asked. But maybe not now; Bart wasn't sure they were ready to hear Horse talk in that people voice again. As if Horse knew what they were thinking, she tossed her mane to one side.

"We'll talk about it," Bart said. "Look, now, here's the city." They stopped, everyone gawking at the skyline of what did seem to be a well-populated place. As they walked through, they approached a big group of gathering folk, kicking up dust from the road as they milled about. Bart hoped there wasn't trouble a brewin'. While they liked to help folk out, they were never looking for trouble. Yet, maybe someone needed help. Best to know. Together, they walked toward them.

"Looks like the courthouse," Tom said. "I'll stay out here."

"Sure, Tom." They looked apologetically at the rest of

the posse. "Doesn't seem like the sort of courthouse that would welcome horses or whiskey neither."

No one said I wanted to go in.

Was that Horse? Bart turned, but Horse wouldn't meet their eye.

Well, fine. Bart adjusted their hat and "pardon"d and "'scuse me"d up to the main doors. "Not in the line, don't worry," they repeated.

A young man—because again in these traditional parts, Bart could usually tell when someone was intending to present a gender—was holding up the line, arguing with an exasperated clerk. Despite the masses outside, it was the only spot at the counter open.

"I don't know what you're asking me to do," the clerk said. "You have a contract. Now, if you could just—" Seeing Bart, the clerk turned toward them. The young man's gaze followed.

"Sheriff!" He rushed over, and in relief the clerk called the next person up. Cheers erupted and people all tipped their hats Bart's way, hollerin' thanks but not wanting to lose their spots in the line.

Bart checked to see if the lad had a pronoun pin, and didn't see one. "No, no," Bart said, "I'm not a sheriff. It's my pronoun pin." They tapped the brass pin. "But I'm a simple folk looking for work, and if your contract fell through, maybe I can help."

The fella glanced at Bart's pin, nodding. "It's not that it fell through, it's that I can't get it to fall through. He / him," the lad added, offering a hand. "Name's Barry."

They shook Barry's hand, but adding a bit of a squint. Bart wasn't interested in bein' part of something unscrupulous. "Tell me about this contract, then."

"I downloaded a BnB app, thinking it would be nice to meet some new people after Ma died."

Bart had heard of these things—like renting, but folk brag about it.

"Problem was, it wasn't people who booked!"

Bart wasn't sure where this was going. An image of a hundred cats popped into their mind, and they shook it off.

"I guess my profile was set to interplanetary. I'm not prejudiced against people who aren't people, mind you, but these ones are just ... well ... whatever planet they're from, I don't recommend visiting it!"

This didn't seem proper. Maybe the clerk had it right. If the folk were staying their own way and just had a different culture, Barry oughta just leave 'm alone.

Barry seemed to notice Bart's hesitation. "No, please, I need you to trust me. It's *awful*."

They still weren't sure. "I don't know what I can do about it. Can't you talk to the company? Ask if they can find them a new room?"

"I've tried. They say they haven't violated any of the terms. They pay on time and they still have another month. Please! I can't last another day."

"If they're within their rights, then they ought to be afforded t'stay," Bart repeated, surprised that the lad wasn't getting it. "Maybe you ought to find a place to go until it's up. Then get off that app," they added.

Barry sighed. "If I could afford to move out, I wouldn't be renting the room in the first place. I've got a job, but Mom saw the doctor a whole lot, and I've got to pay her bills. Some people say I could skip out, but that's not how I mosey."

Bart respected that; maybe he wasn't so bad after all. "Well, folk are normally reasonable. Maybe you can talk to them and just explain it isn't working out."

"They don't understand me." Barry glanced down. "Space talk. I can't figure it out, and it's not on my translate app." He held up his phone.

Well, the posse could help with that. Bart peered through the square courthouse windows, out into the bright street where he could see Horse and Twinkle playing some sort of jumping game.

"Alright, we'll see what we can do. Just understand, these folk sound like they have a full right to be there, so—"

"Thank you, Bart, thank you." Barry moved in as for a hug. Bart held out a hand, stopping him. Folks should not just be hugging strangers like that.

"I was trying to pay the court fee here, to see a judge." He held out some coins. "I could give you that, if you can talk them into leaving."

"We'll see," was all Bart said. They just weren't sure they were comfortable with this whole idea, but then again, they didn't like to see anyone so upset. Maybe they could talk both groups into understanding each other better. Sometimes all a folk needed to do was get to know their fellow folk.

A smell emerged as they neared the small house. Bart covered their nose.

"Yeah, that first. Some fruit from their home world. Smells like rejected barf. It's a shared kitchen, so well, you'll see. Anyway," he pointed, "that side door is theirs."

Bart walked up, resignin' to the smell, and knocked on the side door. As it opened, a large gray blob floated out, hovering in front of them with sort of an undulating beat.

Sort of a sideways octopus, the being was fairly transparent, and clumps of something worked through a tubular system, making a wheezing sound. Wide and round eyes with no eyelids stared, and what looked like three mouths all smacked together in the center, each surrounded by tiny tentacles.

The being started talking, it seemed, by blowing tiny streams of air through a matrix of holes around both eyes, making a spittle-laden whistle sound.

"Oh," Bart said. Well, they weren't tryin'ta be rude. They reached for their translation badge, which had been stuffed in the bottom of the bag after EarthCon, and hit the on switch. There. That should translate them both. Sure enough, the whistles stopped, though Bart tried not to look at the, uh, whistleholes. Maybe that was rude, they rationalized.

"I'm Dan 47982, a he," the being said. "I'm here with my brother, Julie, along with some of our still-forming spawn. We're going to be parents!" One of his tentacles pointed backward. "The spawn are forming in the tub."

Julie squeezed out next to him, holding tentacles full of a goopy green substance, with fibers stretching between each glob. "This is assfruit. It's a delicacy on our world. But, hey, we're on vacay!" He ran it through his mouths with a loud slurping sound then held a tentacle to Bart. "Would you like some?"

Bart tried to offer a polite smile. Actually, who knows whether smiles were polite where they were from. Better to stick with words.

"No, thank you. I wanted to ask you a neighborly question." I mean, this was cutting to the chase a little, but the smell was pungent and Bart's goodwill was not endless. "Barry here, he overcommitted on this room, and was hoping to have use of it sooner."

"We have a contract," Dan said. "We used the app."

"Oh, I know, it's just we're asking if, as a favor you'd be willing to find somewhere else to stay. Earth can be over-rated, you know."

"True," Julie said. "Not the best smelling place."

"*Julie!*" Dan reprimanded.

"Yeah, about that," Bart said. "Anyway, Barry here feels bad about the situation. He'd like to make it up to you. Maybe a partial refund? Or an Earth souvenir?"

Dan leaned forward, bubbles popping in his mouths. "Your excrement is delicious."

"Oh, what?" Bart took a step back.

"We can smell it in the storage unit in the back."

"Packed with nutrients!" Julie added. "It would help our spawn grow strong." He pointed behind with a long tentacle. "We have sprayed them with regurgitated assfruit inside the white basin, but excrement would be more nutritious."

"So you want the . . . excrement. And you'll go?"

All their tentacles contracted with intense grunting and slapping noises. Bart gaped.

"Sorry, that is how we agree. This would be an overly generous trade! Earth is wonderful!"

Bart spied Barry watching from across the lawn. They motioned him over. "Yeah, Barry, Dan and Julie here are great folk. They're willing to leave early, if in exchange they can clean out your outhouse."

Barry stood like a statue.

"I suggest we leave it at that," Bart whispered, and Barry nodded. "Sounds like we've got that all taken care of, then." They were about to pass out from that fruit smell, so it was best to move on.

Just then, Julie craned up, stretching up to peer over Bart's shoulder. "Look, Dan! Look!"

Dan stretched up also, his mouths quivering as he did. "What is this fine beast?" He looked pretty excited. They thought.

Bart turned around—Horse was taking steps backward. "She's not a beast; she's a horse. Named ... Horse. We're friends."

"She's large. Do ... you ride her?" Julie sounded curious.

"No. *No.*" Bart shook their head. Folk could sure be *weird* about horses.

"We meant no offense," Dan clarified. "On our world, these ... horses ... are our rulers. They are small, like *this*"—he held two tentacles close-by—"and they ride us to get where they want to go."

It really was best to be moving along.

"It was nice to meet you," Bart said, moving slowly back toward Horse.

"Wait!" Dan called. "May we pay tribute to your Horse Queen?"

Bart wasn't sure what that meant, but Dan's tentacle stuck into its body and then convulsed outward, holding a tiny diamond-like tiara. "It is sized for our horse rulers, in case one rides us and we can pay them tribute."

"Oh! That's absolutely great," Bart said. "Hey, Horse, look, it can, er, go over your ear."

Horse whinnied what sounded like thanks. Bart took a deep breath and reached out for the little object. They tried not to think about it bein' slippery.

Both Dan and Julie tightened their tentacles together, pointing them in Horse's direction, and chanted something that the translator couldn't quite pick up. Then they released, a puff of powder emanating from each of their eyes.

"Well, we must load the excrement," Dan said. "Thank you again for your visit and generous offer!" Several tentacles vibrating, Julie and Dan closed the door.

"Holy fuck, Bart." Tom was glowing with extra oomph.

Bart couldn't argue that, and stood, mostly stunned, as Barry teetered to their side.

After a long silence, Barry finally spoke. "See, I knew you'd be able to help. Here—" he held out his hands "—the money I offered you."

"Partner, we're just happy to help a folk. Ok, then, we'll be going."

"Wait," Barry said. "Can I get you a shot of whiskey? Anything?"

Old tipped itself over a few times as if urging Bart on.

"Won't say no to that. But, uh, at the tavern? Meet you there in a few."

"Sure thing, friend. There's one just that way. I think I need to . . . stay here and get things cleaned up once they go. You tell Georgie to put you on my tab. And you promise me, if you're ever here again, you'll stop by. You'll always have a friend in the city."

That sure was nice. But it was time to get to that bar. Bart tipped their hat and walked off toward the sunset.

By the time the moon was bright in the sky, Old was full again, and Bart had spent the rest of their own coins on a simple room at a nice inn down the street, because after that they needed a stirred Sazerac and a nice pillow. Tom had gone out ghosting, Old was snuggled into their backpack, fast asleep, and Horse walked out to the park to get some rest in the moonlight.

Tomorrow, they'd have to find some work.

Just Bart: Episode 09

Helping Hands

"In which Bart joins the game . . ."

Bart felt great after that night in the inn. So great, they figured they could take a few days in the city and look for work here. Besides, Horse had been walking day after day since they first met. Let's face it; she'd also been acting stranger and stranger, and maybe a rest would do her good.

The innkeep was friendly to other species, and had directed Horse out to a nice, long backyard with hand-notched wooden fences and even a broad-roofed shelter from the rain and wind.

Bart cut Horse a look as the innkeep brought a bucket of leafy carrots. *I'll bring Chipotle later,* they mouthed, as Horse returned a curt nod.

"Well this oughta fix her up," the innkeep had crowed, clanking the bucket down near the shelter wall.

As for the rest of the posse, Tom hovered in and out, sometimes present and sometimes not. And Old followed Bart around, as it often did, making comments about the city and making sure Bart kept it filled.

"I'm about out of coin," Bart said, getting up to stretch. The sun was streaming in through the window, creating widening rays against the wood plank floor. Smelling a fine earthy musk in the hallway, they wandered out to find a small tray on which rested a stained metal pot of coffee. Happy, Bart poured a cup.

It wasn't just for Old that Bart needed some coin. This inn was right expensive, and the innkeeper'd be expecting payment by the end of tomorrow, for sure.

Well. They better get out and get to work.

Horse was leaping around the backyard, as if chasing an imaginary speck, or a firefly. As Bart knew she'd never hurt a soul, they went to see what she was doing.

Grimacing, they saw Twinkle, the small sprite that their mage friend MageBoss had conjured, giggling and racing in curly loops as Horse raced to catch her.

"Dang, Horse!" Bart called in alarm.

"Oh, they're fine," Old said, zipping into view. "Just playing a game. You can't hurt a sprite, anyway. They're not even real."

"You keep sayin' that," Bart muttered. They were not totally comfortable with this sprite situation. Suddenly, Twinkle popped right between Bart's eyes.

"Hello, Bart! Happy morning!"

"Are you sure you're not real?" Bart squinted. Their eyes weren't getting better with age. "And, could you back up a bit?"

"Sure!" Twinkle spun backward and suddenly Bart could see her tiny face, complete with long eyelashes and wide, upturned lips. "Reality is so subjective!"

"It's not subjective at all," Bart said, frustrated. Maybe they'd need to have a talk with this sprite without Horse listening. "But, anyway, I need to go look for some work."

Horse neighed uncomfortably.

"What ..."

"So," Old started, "since we're in town, um, there's something Horse and I really want to do today."

"Well, you can do whatever you want. I'm going to go out and find some work."

Old tilted a small amount. "We were hoping you'd come with."

"Us," Bart finished.

Old's marker mouth narrowed to a dot. "Sure. Anyway, we're having a game night."

Actually. Game night sounded kind of fun. Bart could get some work in the city, and then meet up wherever their friends were, and—

"It starts in an hour."

"An hour? That's not game night. It's game day."

Old's mouth moved to a line, before popping back again. "Look, are you going to go with us or not?"

"You don't need me, I mean, you could just go."

Old sighed. "So the thing is, this is tabletop. And none of the rest of us have hands. And since there's some specific folk coming, we'd rather keep more on the down low. So maybe you could move the game pieces." Horse stamped a hoof, and her jeweled anklet jingled.

Bart wasn't sure about any of this. "If I'm going to be in the middle of some situation, I'd prefer to know what 'specific folk' are the concern." Bart was a just folk, and if Horse was gaming with outlaws, Bart would at least need to know the type. There were fun outlaws, brave outlaws, and then there were outlaws that a folk just didn't need to support, tacitly or not.

"Jockeys," Old finally mumbled. "The team they are playing is a bunch of jockeys. And no way is Horse going to reveal her true form in front of *jockeys*."

Her true form? What the hell. Bart rubbed their temples. "Look, I don't mean to be difficult, but if you don't want to play against jockeys, then you shouldn't—"

"What, and lose to them?" Old looked like Bart was out of their mind. "This is tournament level; we need to be there."

Tom had popped into view and was floating in ghostly solidarity with the others.

Bart shuffled their boots against the floor. That was some nice pineapple leather. But the fact was, they needed to pay the innkeep. And they sure weren't selling these boots. "I can't. I've got to go get work today."

"Hold on," Old said.

Hold on?

Horse had trotted back into the shelter, then came back out—an innocent look on her face, and the sprite tagging behind.

"So … per monetizes per Twitch channel, and per's definitely broadcasting tonight. Horse texted per, and per's agreed to cut you in."

Per … "Wait a second, is this MageBoss again?"

Old, Horse, and Twinkle all stopped in place as if wounded. "Per's our *friend*," Old whispered.

"Fine, fine. Will it be enough to pay the innkeep?"

Horse snorted.

Old cut her a side look. "It will pay for the inn, and *also* to make sure I get a nice top-shelf refill." Old liked to work in that top shelf, but Bart would buy what they could afford. Still, they trusted their posse. But. One question.

"I'm not saying this is a factor, but I might require some mental preparation." That surely was true. "Horse, will you be … turnin' on your badge?" As they'd found, Horse's EarthCon badge did carry a translation chip, and Horse had just kept it off. It wasn't that Bart objected to the device—Horse could do what she wanted—but Bart did question whether that horsey-talkin' voice she'd had was quite right.

In front of jockeys? No way!

"She says—" Old stopped, with whatever the bottle equivalent of a shrug might be.

"Alright, I'll go." The others cheered. "Now, we don't have to go back to that tower, do we?" Bart had agreed to go, and they'd go, but those magical forests did take a certain amount of energy out of them.

"No," Tom said. "It's the *tournament*, Bart. Right here at the saloon."

Bart brightened a touch. At least it was at the saloon, then. That would be alright.

They walked together—ghost, bottle, sprite, horse, and one slightly nervous but simple folk—to the saloon, Horse almost giddy in the mornin' sunshine. Bart brightened further. Anything that made the posse so happy just couldn't be something to worry about.

And so even Bart was humming a happy tune by the time they walked toward the saloon. No one seemed to mind as the horse clomped up the wood ramp and into the building.

"Gamers?" a young man said, flinging a dish towel over his shoulder. "Back room."

"The back room has a bar?" Bart whispered, but no one answered.

Luckily, it did, and reassuring the bartender they'd be getting coin to pay her back, soon Old was full, Bart was seated at a large round table, and Horse stood behind them, with Tom and Twinkle hovering one over each side.

"Is it weird that it's only us?" Bart asked. "We're in the right place?"

"Totally," Tom answered. "They probably aren't used to people showing up on time."

Bart didn't need to worry. All at once a line of people filed into the room. The first was familiar. Wearing huge purple robes veined with gold and brass embroidery and a proper shiny cap, MageBoss strode in, carrying a massive slushie. Per set it down on the table and then reached out a hand to Bart.

"Good to see you again!" MageBoss said.

Bart almost gasped at the freezing bony fingers that curled around theirs.

"Oop, sorry! Slushie!" per explained, pointing to the drink.

Just then, a large woman with a **she/her** pin swung into the room, wearing a steampunk fascinator. EPIC was tattooed in a curve across her robust chest. She sat next to MageBoss, then leaned across toward Bart.

"Howdy, you must be Bart," she boomed. Instead of offering a shake, she extended her fingers as if tickling the air in their direction. Then she lowered them, yanking a patchwork dice bag from a pocket. "I'm Sal."

"Hi, I'm Bart. Nice to meet you, Sal."

"Don't let us down!" Sal said, chuckling.

Horse rubbed her nose encouragingly against Bart's shoulder, but Bart swatted her back. In a friendly way, o'course.

Just then, three men in three shades of khaki pants appeared in the doorway. One had on a light blue button-down shirt. One wore a neatly striped sweater. And the third, a plain white shirt with a shiny tie. If Bart squinted, they thought the tie had a small D_{20} tie tack. Bart didn't see any pronoun pins, but they felt pretty sure these were men. As if hearing their thoughts, Tom bobbed in agreement.

"Who's ready for a butt whoopin'?" the first man said, exchanging high fives with the other two.

"No one's ever ready for this!" the second man said.

"Mage, who'd you dredge up from that back pond? Ah, couldn't even go to the Enchanted Forest for this one."

"Nope, looks like the sheriff is in town." The three men laughed.

"It's Mage*Boss*," Tom corrected, swooshing around to hover over the table's center. "And no one talks to Bart like that or I'll give you a haunting you'll never forget."

The men didn't react. But something didn't seem right

here. While none of the men were much for bulk, they certainly didn't seem of the build that would be *jockeys.* Horse may have noticed the same thing, as she was unusually still behind them.

"MageBoss," Bart whispered, while the men were bantering between each other, "I thought you told Horse these were *jockeys.*"

MageBoss opened per mouth then closed it. "Oh. I said they were *desk jockeys.*" Per turned to Horse. "I'm sorry, friend. I didn't mean to upset you."

Horse whinnied something that sounded an awful lot like "damn it." Bart craned to peer at her suspiciously, but their neck was a little too stiff to get all the way around and they didn't want to risk pulling it. Necks were sensitive sorts.

"Well, it's ok," Bart said, trying to diffuse the situation. "I'm here now, and um . . ." Bart didn't mean to be rude but the money was important to paying that nice innkeeper. And now the bartender too.

Tom puffed around in front. "You're cutting them in on your Twitch monetization, right?"

MageBoss waved a velvet-trimmed arm. "Yes, yes, I told you I would. Speaking of which." Per tapped the table. "Are we ready to broadcast?"

"Funny, your mom never asks," one man said.

"I'm not really thrilled about gaming with this crew," Bart muttered to MageBoss. "Why would we spend time with people who aren't nice?"

"We're nice, Bart." With Bart's clear expression that

MageBoss knew that's not what they meant, per continued. "Ok, fine. Normally, I'd agree with you. But every round of this tournament has had more views, and this is the final game. The satisfaction of besting these folk in front of thousands of streamers far outweighs having to deal with them for a handful of hours."

A handful of—

"Bart," Sal whispered in a whisper everyone this side o' the mountain could hear. "Let's kick their asses."

"Now, sure, but how did you get this far into the tournament, while me an' the posse were—"

"Bart," Old hissed, sloshing full of whiskey. "You're questioning too much of this. Let's just play."

"Fine," Bart grumbled. They supposed they could—

"Where'd you get that folk hat? Party City?"

Bart snapped their head up to look at the shiny-tied jockey. "Sir, you have yourselves a match. MageBoss. *Broadcast.*" They reached for the glass of whiskey on the old wooden table.

"Hello, Rulers of Ruledom Fancats!" MageBoss called. "Welcome to the tournament finals you've all been waiting for. And we've got a special surprise for tonight! Our game will be played with wizard-fired Wizard Dice, as seen on our recently successful Kickstarter!"

"Haha, I saw that," a man said. "That animated horse on the video looked just like that horse behind you. You probably just scanned it for a model."

A blink later, Horse was behind the three men, her head stuck in between.

"Ah! Get it away."

"You right better call her 'she' and apologize," Bart suggested.

"Fine! Sorry to your weird-ass lady horse!"

Out of nowhere, MageBoss made a series of horsey-sounds. Slowly, not taking her eyes off of them, Horse walked back to their team's side.

Clearing per throat, MageBoss pulled out six sets of dice. A deep firey red, they had metallic engraving, somewhere in between a bronze and a gold. Those were right pretty dice, Bart couldn't help but note.

"As the rules state, only winners keep the dice." Per fished something else out. It was a lone D_{20}, on a tiny carabiner. Dropping her irritation a tiny bit, Horse made a soft sound. "Yes, I thought you would," MageBoss replied. "Here, on your lanyard?"

Horse nodded and MageBoss clipped the iridescent die onto the bottom ring of Horse's sparkly EarthCon lanyard, where it dangled, like a crown jewel, on top of the badge.

Out of a huge sack, MageBoss pulled a large cardboard box. And then another. And then a third. Then a crate of towers. Then a bag of miniatures.

Bart's eyes grew wide.

"Now. Let's get started."

Just Bart: Episode 10

Game Night

"In which Bart's team better win . . ."

The men continued to snicker and taunt as MageBoss unpacked cloth bag after cloth bag of materials.

Horse shook her head behind per, *harrumphing* encouragingly in MageBoss' ear, as per continued setting out the game.

Bart thought about asking what game they'd be playing, but they weren't looking to give the other team the satisfaction of thinking Bart was a noob. Though, if this was the tabletop championship, it was probably something common enough. Something they'd played 'afore.

Then Bart saw the huge box, with the lid propped off to the side. DMV Quest was emblazoned in red font across the side. Bart didn't want to suppose, but they were pretty sure that was just standard Papyrus. Maybe with a drop shadow. But . . . DMV?

"So in six-player, two-team mode, we discard seven cards from stack D after we've reserved three," MageBoss was saying as per set out a stack of wood cubes next to six meeples.

"Sorry, no wooden *horse.*" The three men laughed at their joke. Bart scanned them over again. Blue Shirt seemed to be the quiet one. He'd be the one to watch for strategy.

Sweater did most of the talking; not the sort used to being challenged, Bart could see. And Shiny Tie was all attitude. Bart wasn't worried about him.

Bart felt Horse's hot breath on their neck. For the moment, they ignored it. In fairness, it was Horse that got them into this mess. Bart didn't ask to be here. Old gave them encouraging glances from its place on the table.

MageBoss was going on. "For tournament play, game ends when someone makes it through the door with a working legal document. However, interim documents and registrations have bonus points and effects, so you may want to play for strategy."

Well, that seemed simple enough. So maybe roll dice to move up in line, a little RNG in the luck rolls. A steady mind oughta' play through it. Bart rubbed their hands together. But MageBoss was opening more bags.

Instead of cubes now, per was setting out little plastic gold disks. And gray rectangles. "Where are the reputation markers?" per muttered.

"Now'a—" Bart leaned in so the other team wouldn't hear. "How complicated is this endeavor?" Old grimaced.

"Have you ever been to the DMV?"

Well, now. Bart couldn't say that they had. When they'd lived in the city, their trusty bicycle had been all they ever needed. And their sturdy feet. Bart glanced down to admire their pineapple leather boots.

"Bart." Per interrupted their thoughts. "You are going to have so much fun."

"That's what your mom always says," Shiny Tie crowed.

That was enough of that.

Tom swung around in front, but Bart waved him back. They had this.

"Now I'd never assume the makeup or gender of one's guardianship, legal or assumed," Bart started. Sweater snorted. "But if any of you does have a mom who still graces this here land, I can't imagine she's having too much fun crying while she thinks about what a disrespectful child she now has."

Sal cut Bart a side glance, then leaned forward on the table, drawing the men's attention. "By the end of this game, you'll call *me* Mommy."

"Anyway!" MageBoss glanced around nervously, as a tall woman sauntered in. "With the Judge here, let's review the house interpretation of the rules. By house I mean what was settled at TournaCon."

See, Bart was not about to subject any reader of this here serial to the drama that ensued over the next forty minutes. Horse stamped back and forth, Old lost some of its whiskey, and even Tom shrunk back into a corner. At first, Bart was confused why MageBoss had brought a novel to read if they were here in a game tournament, until they realized it was the rule guide for DMV Quest. A guide that MageBoss consulted frequently, muttering and consulting with Sal as per lifted up per jeweled reading glasses to decipher the fine details. Bart was then informed about time tracking, reputation scoring, document augmentation, more stuff than they even want to remember.

"The interference rules got me a bit perplexed," they said in a low voice.

MageBoss looked like Bart didn't get it at *all*. "That's the point, Bart, Dynamic game play. Interference points *change* the game's rules, they're changing the texture of gaming. You should try campaign mode."

Bart squinted.

"Now everyone place their meeples in the parking lot. Roll to see order of parking spot selection."

"What if I walked?" Bart asked.

As MageBoss explained the luck ranges on a D120 for sidewalk placement, Bart gave in. "I'll just roll for a spot."

Bart still had no idea what they were doing. But as they were mostly following instructions from MageBoss—move here, roll this, play this, Bart seemed to be getting along.

There were times, though, they'd think this game must be about over, then they'd re-look at the game board and realize they were still back in the line. Beyond that, they'd get a card played and have to go to the car for another document, or need to use the bathroom, then after using the bathroom, they had to convince the check-in folk that—anyway, Bart was thinking this might be a *real* long game. But, MageBoss had promised that the livestream was monetized, and that Bart would be able to pay the innkeep for sure, whether they won or lost.

Shiny Tie sucked some sort of nacho chip powder off his fingers, then picked up one of the cards.

Actually, they were going to win.

Bart felt like they'd reached a new age in their life when the game finally looked ready to conclude. Issue was, it was close as a close-talkin' co-worker. Bart got ready to move up their meeple.

"You can't do that," Blue Shirt said.

"It says if my number is up, I can approach the desk, as long as no other card was played."

"A card *was* played. My augmentation card from last round had the ability to last two rounds."

"The ability, sure. But you didn't invoke it."

"Don't have to."

Now, Bart had seen the text on the card. It was a clear conditional. If someone played an interrupt, then they could declare that the card lasted another round.

"An interrupt was played, and—"

Simply put, this was cheating. "An interrupt was *not* played," Bart said. "You blind discarded then shuffled the deck."

"It was an interrupt."

"Even if so, you didn't declare it."

Sal cranked around to find the Judge. She was tapping her chin.

"MageBoss, may I see that guide?"

Now, see, Bart aged another lifetime or two while the Judge consulted the rules, and Sweater and Sal threw back and forth arguments for their case.

This here saloon was about to become a cultural site, and Bart's preserved body would be mistaken for a hopefully handsome mannequin at the table before this game was going to end.

Bart was looking at the clock and not only was it gettin' real late, but Bart was right sure it had been an hour since the question had been raised. *Only* an hour. Must be some sorta' time dilation involved. Old was right near empty, so much it was pretty much just sitting there.

"I yield."

Everyone's face snapped up. Blue Shirt. Sweater. Shiny Tie. Sal. MageBoss. The Judge. Even Old mustered enough to turn its marker mouth into a tiny 'o' as Bart ignored Horse's breath behind them.

"I yield," Bart said. "This isn't important. Let's continue on." Bart grabbed up the red dice (there were three sets) and started to shake them in their hands.

MageBoss turned to the Judge.

She shrugged. "Their call."

The men all laughed in unison. Shiny Tie held his hand out, and noting that Sweater was still gloating at Bart, Blue Shirt rushed to slap it.

"Good. I was tired of waiting in this shithole anyway," Sweater said.

"Oh, I don't know, it seems nice here," Bart said.

Sweater smirked. "Nice in an ugly-ass horses sort of way." Shiny Tie held out his hand, then lowered it as the others chortled.

Behind Bart, the breath paused. They smiled politely. "So anyway, that's a setback for me. Looks like I'll lose a turn waiting for the numbers to rotate. I suppose the staff was listening to all that." They turned to MageBoss, giving per a long look.

"A turn is all we need," Blue Shirt said, as he moved his tokens up front to the desk. "I've got everything I need right here. Reputation. Documents. Ten forms of ID. Gold coins.

Matching number. Luck score. Stamina. Bladder on green. I'm ready to check out."

The silence was long and Bart wondered whether MageBoss had understood. One thing Bart got from the rules was, the player who made the move couldn't call a challenge. Only another player.

It was Sal who smacked down a stack of cards. "Challenge. I call challenge. The clerk at the desk just heard the other team call her an ugly-ass horse. No way she is going to process that paperwork. Back of the line. Sorry I'm closed. Citation. Smoke break. Something."

Bart beamed at their teammate as the Judge stepped forward, tapping her chin.

"That's crap," Sweater said. "No one even said that. I mean, that comment was out-of-game." He pointed to Horse, who was making a tiny rumbling noise.

"He didn't call a time-out. You had resumed play. Completely in-game in my view, of course, that's if you agree, Judge." Sal leaned back and twisted toward the Judge.

"You cannot do this," Sweater stated with a lilt.

The Judge's eyebrows twitched a hair, and Bart was feeling that this was about to be very . . . very . . . just.

"I'm sorry. The clerk finds that there is a mark on the signature. Therefore the signature has been tampered with. She's not comfortable issuing docs on what could be a fraudulently tampered-with signature."

"We have all the documents!" Shiny Tie jumped from his seat. "We have reputation! This is *horseshit!*"

Everyone grew silent, and Blue Shirt threw his head into his hands.

"I'm sorry. The document is void. Team MageBoss, do you have documents for the clerk?"

Quietly, Bart gathered all the tokens, stacked their cards, and set their three meeples on top. "Yes. Thanks so much for helping us today. We have everything right here. It's just enough for one standard license, but I believe with your help we can get this issued and make it to the door? We really appreciate your help."

The Judge checked the cards … sort of … and smiled. "This all looks in order. And since Team Bee-aches can't make it to the door next turn nor can they throw an obstacle or turn interference characteristics, that means Team MageBoss wins."

Horse's snort was so enthusiastic, Bart nearly fell from their chair. Then again, with her hooves stomping on the shaking hollow floor, they moved aside by a good stick's width.

"How was that for an exciting finish?" MageBoss was saying into per webcam. Well, heck, Bart had forgotten that thing was even on. "I hope you'll join me in two days, where I'll be joined by Horse, Old, Tom, Sal, and Tameka for another great game."

As per clicked off the broadcast, the Judge walked over with three glittering medals. Sal bowed as she slipped it over her head and onto her chest. MageBoss couldn't hide per grin as per medal was lowered onto per purple robes. And just as the Judge reached Bart, they reached up and held the brim of their hat. "I think I know someone who might just enjoy this medal."

Horse threw her front hooves onto the table, rattling the game pieces as MageBoss scrambled to slide them back into the bags.

"I can't reach up there," the Judge said, and settling down a touch, Horse lowered back to the floor and dipped her head. The medal rested neatly within Horse's sparkly lanyard, on which dangled both her EarthCon badge and her new wizard fire wizard-fired D_{20}.

They stayed quiet as the other team flung up from their chairs, turned, and stomped out. Bart would normally think thoughts about a team that didn't help pick up, but they were just glad to have them gone.

Everyone seemed some combination of content or worn out as they put away the game pieces, and the Judge was nice enough that she brought Old back, fully filled. Old winked at Bart and they didn't even bother to ask it what it'd talked the lady into filling it with. Then MageBoss handed Bart and Sal each a big bag of coins, as Tom peered on. Bart didn't bother to count it; this was more than they'd seen in quite a while. Apparently the money was all in games.

Sal made some comment about being a big hugger, so Bart let her squeeze them up into a huge hug—no need to talk about that more, but it's fine, she was nice—and MageBoss sighed with a big nod. After a side conversation with Horse that did seem a little terse but ended with Twinkle spraying imaginary glitter around them both, MageBoss shuffled back out of the door, leaving the posse in the empty room alone.

"Sorry," Tom said. "We thought they were jockeys."

"It's fine," Bart said with a yawn. "Let's just stick to tournaments with nicer folk next time."

Fortunately, everyone agreed.

Tired, Bart didn't even stop by the bar. Instead, they dragged on back to the room, Old floating behind. But there was one more stop to make.

"Mx?" they said, politely, into the main office.

The innkeep offered a warm smile. "I hope you're enjoying your stay."

Bart tipped their hat. "I sure am. But . . . I have something for you." They held out a bag, full of coins. "This should pay for what I owe, plus another week, and also something extra for your trust and hospitality."

"Why thank you, Bart. Now, I do have a question. I'm making a cheesecake in the kitchen. My own blend of vanilla, lemon, silken tofu, and cashew cream, with a coconut milk lime icing. If I were to bring up a fresh slice for you later, would you be interested?"

Maybe Bart wouldn't go to sleep quite yet. They glanced at Old.

"That sure would be nice." Then, they remembered Horse out in the yard. "Would it be possible . . . to get two? I'll pay for the second."

The innkeep gave a swift shake of the head. "Two will be just fine. Now I'll see you later."

Bart nodded, then shut the door behind them.

Just Bart: Episode 11

Old's Party

"In which Old sees some friends ... "

Bart slept in again; they were going to have to stop getting used to that. Luckily, though, after paying the innkeep from the money MageBoss had given them, they could go a couple more days without having to worry about finding work. Any day a folk didn't have to worry about knowing if they could pay for their next meal was a great one. They wondered what folk did with their time who didn't have to worry every day.

Stretching, they walked over and opened the curtains on the second-floor window, overlooking the main street of the city. Sometimes the city looked like a lot of things, but right now it looked rather plain. People walked by, ushering their children, taking care of their life, or just working their legs before they had to sit down a long stretch.

They better not get used to city life, though. There was no way they could afford this room more than the days they'd been here. Besides, the city could be harsh. Sometimes a person could get lost and feel like even in a big crowd, no one cared about them. Bart's journey kept them moving away from all that.

Horse and Tom seemed in no hurry to go; they had lots of friends and contacts here, and Bart had right given up on figurin' what they were up to half the time. Especially with Horse sleeping outside; it seemed she went wherever she wanted. Maybe one horse could get lost in the big city too. Unlike Bart, Horse seemed to enjoy it.

Old was snoozing away on the side of the bed, its little marker mouth wavering back and forth in a tiny snoring rhythm.

Bart could understand that; it was a right comfortable bed. Yet, soon, it would be time to go.

After a warm shower and a lightly-sweetened coffee, Bart felt ready to face another day. They jumped, seeing Old was already hovering before them.

"Old, what's up?" Bart groaned. "I'm barely through my coffee."

"We're not leaving the city, are we?" It spun around in concern.

"Soon, Old. I've been enjoying this room a bit, but this place isn't me. I've got to be me."

In all of Old's distress, its level of whiskey seemed to lower a bit.

"Running away isn't you either, Bart."

Grumbling, Bart reached back for the coffee. "You're a free . . . bottle, Old."

"We're friends. You know that."

"I know." They tried to offer Old a smile, but Old was bouncing around again. "What? There's something."

"Well there's a party in town tonight. I think we should go."

"A party? 'We?' What sort of party?"

Old's eyes flipped off to an angle as if rolling them. "Just a party with some of my friends. Come on, Bart, it'll be great."

Well, Bart figured, a city party would have a lot of people, and it couldn't be that everyone would avoid them this time. Old seemed so excited. But, see, Old didn't always understand about all the types of people. The sorts that could make friends easily, and the people that were kind and the others who weren't and all of it. What it was like for a folk to feel alone.

It bopped up and down, anticipation drawn onto its face. Old didn't really ask for too much.

"Oh, alright, I'll go. But it's still early in the day and I need to see if I can find some work."

"I thought you made some money!"

Bart shook their head. "Sure, but how long does one payment last? Even a nice one. When you make the choice to wander, you live with that choice every day."

"Do you regret it?"

"Nah," they whispered, pulling together their things and heading out into the city.

What a mess. One person said Bart was too expensive, a person who Bart knew had the money to pay them right. Another said they weren't sure about the quality of their work, which Bart knew was just another way to say they didn't want to pay a fair rate. A third said they'd love to hire them, but didn't provide much for specifics.

By the time they dragged back to the room, they were right ready for that party.

One glass of whiskey would be nice. Before leaving. "I've got to get out of here," they muttered at the wall. They were starting to feel tired.

"Come on, Bart. You said we'd go." Old's label looked extra shiny tonight, though it was torn as it'd always been. As long as Bart had known it anyway.

"Horse and Tom? And, er, Twinkle?" Bart had *not* been convinced that sprite was ethical, whatever Horse said about her.

"They're . . . elsewhere." Old glanced to the side.

Fine, if it wanted to cover for whatever better party Horse and Tom had gone off to, Bart didn't need to worry.

"Playing pool," Old continued.

What? How did . . . Anyway.

The party was occurring across three houses, as it turned out, with crowded patios in between each. Bart could see people from behind the hedges, mingling over the sound of the music. "I don't know, Old. This looks like far too much party for me."

"Well if you want to go back . . ." Old's little eyes bent into arcs.

"Oh, let's go." Bart adjusted their belt and hat and took a deep breath that ended up shallow.

The commotion took them back. Old wasn't kidding about the party being its friends. Bottles floated—and sometimes rolled—around. Bart had to watch their steps to avoid bumping into anyone. People were there too, but they all seemed to be guests of the bottles, just like Bart had been invited by Old.

Loud music was blaring across the space. Bart preferred being able to actually talk; otherwise what was the point? At least it seemed to be a 90's mix, which was fine with them. "Legend of a Cowgirl" came on next. Even for folks who called a woman a girl, Bart sure wasn't a woman, and they had no idea why anyone would exploit a cow when cashews and guacamole existed, but it was a nice song and Bart liked it just fine.

A bottle of tequila floated by. "Howdy," they said to the person who wafted up behind it. Without a pronoun pin, Bart felt she was signaling female. They tapped their own brassy pin: **they/them** in proud display. "I'm Bart. And this here is Old."

"Oh, heeey," she said, continuing to walk past. Well.

They tried again, this time with a tall man. Bart wasn't sure about the read on this guy, but they'd been wrong before, so they'd try and be friendly. He was big but his bottle was small; a standard beer bottle. Mexican label, Bart noted.

"Howdy," they said, tipping their hat to the pair. "I'm Bart and this is Old."

"Hola," the cerveza replied. "Este tipo," it sighed, tipping a bit to point to the man.

"What's up?" he called out. "Old Bart? Fuck yeah! Hey, looks like you brought the good stuff." Bart glanced around, expecting Tom to show up, but they remembered he was out with Horse.

"Let's go," Old whispered in Bart's ear, with an apologetic glance to the cerveza. "If you need an out, let me know."

"I'm fine; he'll forget where he set me anytime now, then whoops! Where'd it go?" The bottle grinned.

They walked into the next room, well Bart walking and Old floating as it did. Now, here was a familiar sight. A fine, tall bottle of scotch. It had been a while.

Bart introduced themself to the bottle as well as the portly folk who accompanied it.

"Where are you from?" the scotch asked. "I'm Speyside."

"What?" Old tilted a bit.

"Where are you distilled?"

Old narrowed its eyes. "I've been refilled a lot, so who knows? Even originally, I'm not sure. My label's been torn a long time." It shook a little, drawing attention to the torn label from which only the word **Old** could be clearly read.

"Some of the blends are very affordable," the bottle said. Bart glanced over to the person, who seemed distracted.

"Have you been on any tours?"

Bart wasn't sure how to answer that—their whole life was a tour—but Old was rushing from the room and so Bart followed.

They almost ran into quite a crowd. "Oh, sorry," they said. Bart did have to stop apologizing. They'd give Angel credit; that was one thing she'd said a lot.

Three thin bottles of vodka were engaged in lively chatter, surrounded by a whole group of people. One of the bottles proudly wore a bright yellow lemon. Another was wrapped in rainbow packaging.

"It's Pride Vodka!" someone said. "*Mmm*," Bart nodded politely. The conversation wasn't bad, though. One of the women liked one of the other women at their school, and Bart couldn't keep up with about six names involved, but it sounded like a whole lot of drama.

They tried to keep out of drama whenever they could. Not that it worked. Glancing around, they saw two wide bottles float over.

"Hey!" one said.

"Uh oh." Old had spun right over to Bart's face.

"No Schnapps."

"What?" Now that wasn't right to be prejudiced against a folk by their variety.

"Bad Karaoke, Bart, I know what you're thinking. You take it all too far! Peach is bad enough, but look—Hot Damn. Cinnamon! Yeah, so pleasant. Like sweet breakfast buns or grandma's candy. Except if grandma's candy *wrecked* you for three days. You wouldn't talk to it again either. Come on, we gotta go."

Old was getting outta control. Bart peered over to see how it was doing. Its magic, or whatever you called it, used up the whiskey inside. No matter how much coin Bart earned to keep it full, it was always out again.

Hot Damn floated over. Images of flames flared across its label. "You wanna party?"

Old was right up in their face now, making the best little marker grimace Bart had ever seen. "Alright, buddy. This is my friend Bart and they've got a companion."

"No thanks," Bart said, with a side glance to Old. Hot Damn didn't leave though, and kept following them outta the room. Which was not right. I mean, why couldn't it have stayed with the lemon vodka? They figured that would be right pleasant.

"Go!" Old urged.

They ducked into a side room, trying to find a little space.

A not so flashy person was leaned back against a couch. Bart was delighted to see a **she/her** pin—how considerate—and they tapped their own pin.

"Bart. And this is Old."

"Nice to meet you, Bart. This is Gin. And I'm not important."

Gin wasn't floating around all out of control like Old was. It was sitting politely on a small table, with a tall martini glass to its side. Oh, with a twist of lemon rind. Well that was nice.

"Hi, Gin. This is Old. It's a whiskey bottle. And I don't know you—" they turned to the person "—but I do know you're important." Bart didn't like to contradict a folk, but this was something serious. "Every person is important."

"Sounds like a slogan," she said.

"It sounds like a slogan because companies say stuff like that to make us feel good about what they're selling. And that's alright, as long as they mean it and act like it too. Or it sounds like a slogan because regular folk don't say it more often. You're important."

They knew the look in her eyes. They'd felt it too. Bart hadn't been feeling important themself today. But maybe they could help someone else.

"I guarantee you. You are important."

She smiled, still a bit unsure.

"See. You just proved it. I was feeling out of place here, and that smile just helped me. Since you're important to me right now, that proves you're important. And I bet it's more than just that."

The woman laughed. "You know what," she said, "I like your logic. Not sure about this party, though."

Old had wanted to be here, so they stayed polite and kept quiet.

"Hey, Bart," Old said. "Maybe I'm getting, well, you know, but I'm not so into this either. Maybe that's been enough of a night. Perhaps for you both. What do you think?" It turned to the woman.

"I suppose I'm ready to go." She started fumbling with the martini glass. "This is their glass," she nodded to the side, "but this little marker came with the bottle. With Gin." She held out a little piece of metal, curved into an almost closed circle, from which dangled a tiny chain of little crystals, along with a fancy H charm. The logo for the brand, they supposed.

"That's pretty," they said, admiring the way it caught the flickering light from the old-fashioned lamp.

"It's a gift," Gin said from the table. "Gift sets were the same price as regular, since I'd been sitting around since New Year's and the seller thought I was taking too much room on the shelf. She's already got one of these, and we were just talking about who might enjoy this one."

"Would you like it?" She held it out, letting it swing from her finger.

"I'm not much for sparkly things—at least most of them—but I have a friend who would love that," they admitted. It was true, and they both seemed to want to find the trinket a home. Old nodded enthusiastically, and Bart knew it was thinking the same thing.

"Perfect," the woman said, handing it to Bart, then rising from the couch, Gin following along.

"Maybe I'll see you again," she said. "Would be nice to have a friend."

"I don't think I'm staying in the city," Bart managed to get out.

"Oh," she said. "It was nice to spend a little time with you. I've enjoyed it a great deal."

"Thanks," Bart said. "Maybe there's still a little time. Why don't we get a glass of water first? There's a place down the street that has great late-night fries. Vegan fryer too." Bart couldn't handle the idea of perfectly fine potatoes bouncing around with parts of a bird. Folk just made no sense.

"I'd like that," she said. "You seem real nice and I wish that we could be friends. But I really shouldn't stay up. Gotta get out and find work in the morning." She sighed, tipping back the rest of the martini glass before setting it on the table.

"Yeah," they said, knowing how that felt. "Me too."

They walked outside together, and Bart didn't miss the sounds of the party as they wandered down the quiet street.

Bart was going to need to get out of the city pretty soon. But it was good to remember, there were folk everywhere who were nice. Folk that needed friends. They were glad they'd met. And with that thought in mind, they wandered back to their room, latching the door behind them and taking a moment to get that glass of water.

They glanced down at Old, who had already fallen asleep on the bed.

"Good night, Old." They paused. "One of these days, I think things will be ok."

No one answered. And Bart drifted off to sleep.

Just Bart: Episode 12

An Unusual Town

"In which Bart leaves the city . . . "

That party reminded Bart what happened the last time they stayed too long in a city.

It was time to go.

Moseyin' around the nice, homey room kept so lovely here at the inn, they did have a pang of regret for what it felt like to have a cozy, comfortable bed, and someone to make sure there was fresh coffee.

That just wasn't the cards Bart had been dealt.

Head sagging a bit, they went out to tell Horse. They were pretty sure she'd argue, but instead she looked worn. She was even eating a bucket of saggy carrots, and who knew how long those had been out.

Tom was slumped down near her. Bart didn't think a ghost actually had to rest against anything, but perhaps that was ghost business.

Was that sprite still here? At least the sprite would be peppy. They saw her, hovering around Horse, but her glitter wasn't really even multi-colored today, it was more like gray dots, sleepily wafting in her wake.

The gray dots looked sort of cool.

For a second, they hesitated to tell everyone. They'd

almost lined up a few jobs, here, talking to folk around town. Maybe they should stay a while longer.

They took another look at the posse. 'Cept Old. Old wasn't even here; it was still laying upstairs, conked out on the side table. If the city was so great, then why'd they all look like this?

"I'm fixing to leave, if you'd like to join me."

Tom rose up, trailing to Bart's side. They were never sure what to do with that ghost; if there were some type of rules for appropriate handling of ghost companions, Bart wasn't read into them. Horse made a gruff noise, and took a step toward them.

"Oh!" Bart remembered what they'd brought from last night. Fumbling in their pocket, they pulled out the small metal charm with the sparkling crystals and the fancy H. The H stood for whatever brand of gin gave the promotion, but they had to admit, they'd thought of Horse when they saw it.

"Would you like this, Horse? I thought you could clip it around the edge of your ear."

Horse perked right up, her metal and dice and badge and other jewelry all jangling as she pranced over.

"Now, you know I'm not so tall," Bart reminded, and Horse, with an apologetic shake of her head, lowered it, so Bart could reach her ear. Carefully, they wiggled the charm around one side, where it rested comfortably. "Any pinch?"

Horse shook her head.

"You know, you're a free horse. You don't have to follow me."

Making some even gruffer horsey noise, she looked right offended.

"Horse loves you!" Twinkle chastised.

Now, hold up. The sprite was now talking? This had all gone too far outta' hand.

"Of course I talk. If she's a free horse, then I'm a free sprite. And are we your posse or not?"

"Sure," Bart said. "A posse of five."

Now they both looked offended.

"Five? No four," Twinkle said. "I'm not totally real. I'm just with Horse. So it's still just four."

This was way too weird. But Bart's head wasn't totally clear either. "Well, I'm going to pack my bag and get a bit more coffee. Then I'll say goodbye to that real nice innkeep, and I'll be back this way."

Tom followed Bart back inside, making a show of floating through the walls rather than using the doors. "You mind folks' privacy," Bart said.

Tom gave them a disgusted look.

Saying farewell to the nice innkeep was the hardest part, but after a bit, they were ready to go. Not to say it took so long to pack one messenger-style bag, but maybe Bart could confess to stalling just a little bit longer.

No. They'd made up their mind. Time to go.

"When we get to the next town, I'll need to actually get some steady work, and keep it for a few days." Bart wanted to make sure they were clear. No more getting the carts derailed by ex-folk and mages and whatever else they tended to run into. I mean, they weren't trying to boss anyone around, but searching for coins was a necessity Bart couldn't avoid.

"Horse wants to make a stop first," Twinkle said.

Old, who was bopping around to the side, now bounced around in front. "Oh, she's leveled up! How wonderful!"

Now, Bart didn't know what in Prince's great nation this posse was talking about, but more relevant was what stop Horse was proposin'. "Horse, what are you thinking?"

"It's just a side town," Twinkle answered. "Not on the road, but, well don't worry yourself with those details. As long as you're willing, it'll be a quick stop. Unless, of course, you'd like to try it for work. There is a *lot* of money in this town."

"Now, how am I supposed to do this?" Bart squinted. "Do I talk to Horse, or to Twinkle?"

"Same thing!" Twinkle answered. "Please don't be so uptight."

A small growl escaped Bart's lips. They were not one to be looking for trouble. Fact was, they'd heard that part about all the money. Oh, who were they to tell Horse no. Horse was a good friend. "Sure. Just let me know where we ought to be headed."

"We can just keep going this way," Twinkle said.

Sure enough, within a while a side path emerged and Horse turned to walk down it. Again, there was something suspicious about all this, but Bart followed along.

Along the horizon, a series of hills emerged, well, Bart hadn't known there were hills this way. And then, in between those hills rose huge metal spires, buzzing with activity and energy like something right out of one of those science fiction periodicals. Angel always liked those, they remembered with a smile.

Bart wasn't going to try and play around. Horse had done something weird again, and this wasn't a standard town. "Alright, Horse. And Twinkle. Whatever. Tell me what this is."

"Future Town," Twinkle answered.

"Are there, you know, folk here?" It seemed a valid question given the gleaming metallic spires. Their parents always said the machines were going to take over, and maybe this was it.

"Not humans. Just Horses and Robots."

Old waggled. "Cool!" It seemed excited. "Maybe one of those robots could print me a new label."

"Do you want a new label?" Bart felt bad. If they'd known that, they could have tried to get one painted or something.

"No! It was just an idea. I like me how I am. Tom, did you see that?"

Tom did seem to see it; he was glowing brighter than Bart had seen him in days.

"Horses and Robots! Awesome." Tom floated on ahead, excitement brimming in his ghostly swing.

"Now, again, why are we here?"

"Oh, sorry, she didn't tell you?" Twinkle looked apologetic. "Horse has a dentist appointment, and she didn't want to miss it. You know how far ahead you have to make those things."

Bart did know.

"We'll be off this way," Twinkle said. "Tom wants to go with us; he loves asking the dentist questions."

"Ok." Bart went to the dentist when they needed to, but 'love' was not an emotion they brought with them. 'Appreciate', sure.

As Horse trotted away, Bart had a sudden worry. "Wait, how will we connect back?"

"We'll find you," Tom called behind him.

Soon it was just Bart and Old again. "Best we get some work," Bart said.

Old didn't answer. It tended not to when Bart was looking for work; that was fine.

Now, they wondered what sort of work a folk could get in a city full of Horses and Robots.

"Please clarify behavioral training credentials," the clerk said.

"What? I mean, I'm sorry I don't know what that refers to. Specifically," they added.

"Subject may be from digital era; evaluate," another voice chimed in.

"I will ask them," the robot said.

Bart wasn't sure what their behavior had to do with any of this, but if robots were this respectful of a folk's pronoun, they might have to meet some more robots.

"Bart," the clerk tried again. "Do you operate in coding paradigms? Do you know any programming languages?" The voice was modulated to sound kinder.

"No, I'm a simple folk. I'm good at construction, and helping out with tasks." The robots exchanged glances.

"Are you beneath manure removal? Would this opportunity offend you?"

Bart couldn't say they were thrilled by the idea.

"Standard wage applies for all organic tasks. Manure removed at one hundred coins an hour."

That settled that.

Soon, Bart was walking up and down the streets of Future Town with a shovel and a cart, Old humming a little tune beside them. The robots had offered them a scooter so they didn't have to walk, but Bart had politely declined. Scooters.

Bart didn't much care for the fragrance of the manure, but they'd sure had worse jobs. And so they tipped their hat to horses and robots passing by and spent the day feeling happier than they had in a while.

The thing with horse manure is by the time a folk gets to one end of the street, the dung is back on the other side. But the work was per the hour, and Bart had plenty of coins now to fill Old, get some supper, and even find a room.

They still hadn't run into Horse, but maybe they could find where the dentist was. "Howdy," Bart said, approaching a horse. The horse neighed.

"Says the name is Horse," Old said. Old had a thing for understanding horses, Bart had learned.

But that wasn't Horse. Course, people folk could sometimes have the same name.

"Bart, all the horses here are named Horse," Old clarified. "Keeps things simple."

"What about the robots?"

Old chuckled, its little marker face shaking with amusement. "You couldn't pronounce their names if you tried. Even I can't."

Alrighty. "Can you ask Horse if there's a dentist around these parts?"

"Several," Old answered. "I think we're going to have to wait for Horse to find us. But in the meantime . . ."

Bart looked at the sun, which was still a bit overhead for their comfort. But they'd thought of something. "If this is a town full of horses, wouldn't there have to be horse stores?"

Old gasped.

"Old, now you know me better than that. I mean, stores to buy the sort of things horses like."

Old's eyes had narrowed.

"Again, you know what I mean. Not regular horses; that's mostly grass. I'm talking about fancy horses like Horse. You know how she likes gifts."

Spinning around, Old lit right up. "That's a great idea. She sure is fancy! That's why we get along." It drew a little hand on itself that pointed to the label. Bart tried not to consider that was weird. "I used to be fancy too."

"Oh, you're still fancy, Old." Bart couldn't miss Old's grin of pure delight. They watched the horses walking by, and considered asking one for advice. "Yeah. These horses'll tell her," they muttered to the bottle. "I just sense it."

Old didn't argue.

"Let's ask one of them there robots about a gift shop. Um, pardon us?"

Bart remembered that maybe they should have specified

a price range to that robot, because this turned out to be the most expensive damn gift shop Bart had ever seen. *How do horses get so much money?* They grumbled it to themself because they didn't want to be rude. Instead, they walked up and down the grass aisleways as an aggressive saleshorse followed them extolling the virtues of each piece through a hovering translator bot. Like that EarthCon badge, this bot also spoke in a fake horsey voice, and Bart could barely take it. But what to get her?

Horse already had an anklet. And an earring. And a fancy bow. And a tiara. Bart sighed.

"Oooh, how about some unicorn hair?"

"Eww," Bart was unable to stop from popping that out. Well, maybe this hair was synthetic, but even so, that seemed a bit of a control factor that Bart couldn't—

"Oh, no, no. It's just a term for the product. No unicorns involved. See, look." The bot clipped onto a long stream of pastel, shimmery, multi-colored hair and held it carefully up. "It clips into the tail. Or you can wear it wherever. For the more avant-garde."

Bart didn't know if Horse was avant-garde, but she sure would like that hair.

By the time Bart had fished out enough coins to pay for the thing, the bag was almost empty. Guess that meant another day of shoveling the shit. Oh, well. Horse was important. And there was still enough to get through today.

With the hair carefully wrapped in what the saleshorse, Horse, bragged to be eco-friendly tissue paper, Bart sauntered back out onto the street. They glanced around.

Horse still wasn't back. Yet Old was staring at them with beady marker eyes.

"Ok, Old. We can go. But do robots even have bars?"

Hell if Bart was going to ask about a horse bar. They'd seen Horse's party after all.

"Just robot bars," Old answered. "Unless you're interested in a horse bar."

"About those robot bars, they're still . . . a bar? A tavern? The old waterin' hole? Or is it some grease and oil thing?"

Old's face shook side to side. "I guess you've never met a robot. Robots do nothing *but* drink. They just don't let it on to the humans."

"You're lettin' it on to me."

Old smiled. "Well I'm not a robot, and you're better than human. You're Bart. Now, come on. I could use a refill myself."

Just Bart: Episode 13

Robot Bar

"Bart might as well stop in . . ."

Bart trusted Old on which bar to try. Trustin' a magic whiskey bottle on which robot bar to try started to feel a little like Bart was losing grip, but they just weren't ready to deal with that yet.

So they walked on in.

Bart didn't know how robot folk would take to human folk waltzin' into their bar on a' evening such as this, but no one seemed to pay much mind as they strolled in and took a look around.

For a minute, Bart worried this was one of those fancy bars with expensive drinks and colored lights behind all the bottles. Then they realized robots have colored lights as a matter of course, and actually it seemed pretty laid back.

"Pardon me," they said, tipping their hat to a passing robot. "Am I welcome here, and if so, would I wait to be seated?"

"You are welcome, Bart. Sit where you'd like. Do not defecate on the floor."

They had to catch themself a moment, but the robot had already moved along. "That robot knew my name," Bart remarked, to Old, they supposed.

"Yeah. They're all networked in. Facial recognition.

As soon as you talk to one of them, everyone knows. Unless there's some sort of ban or off-grid situation. One thing I've learned after a lot of years of being a whiskey bottle is you do *not* want to engage in robot politics."

"Well, alright. So, where do you think we should sit?" Bart normally preferred the bar, but they didn't know if there was robot etiquette they needed to mind. The robot had said sit wherever. Old didn't answer, as though it knew Bart was working through all that and would just go sit at the bar anyway.

They walked toward the bar, a steel structure that Bart was surprised to see looked a lot like the wooden bars they were used to, except this one had red paint stripes in what might have been a robot language. Maybe it said something cool, like a funny bar joke. Bart still had their messenger bag, and they were wearing their hat. They hoped hats weren't rude here. After working outside all day an' sweating a bit, they were feeling pretty self-conscious about what their hair would look like at this point. These robots probably had all sorts of sensors, though. Maybe it didn't matter.

A spherical bot with little hanging legs buzzed by, two lights, like eyes, staying locked on Bart. They decided to keep the hat on.

The bar was pretty crowded, and they weren't going to use up a space for two folk, so they sat near the end, on a single stool. Robots sat to each side. One was downing a large pink drink through a rubbery-looking straw, and to the other side, one had a pitcher of what looked like a margarita. Bart tried to see if they had anyone they were sharing it with, but the bot looked alone. Well, then, one of those pitcher of margaritas nights. Bart felt a connection to this one, and figured they'd start there.

"Howdy," they offered, tipping their hat. "Do you mind if I sit here?"

The robot was silver and mostly canister shaped, with lights and ports covering a lot of the surface. Two rolling tracks were retracted up against the sides, allowing the bot to sit. The design was clearly meant to roughly evoke human features, in the sense the robot had a small canister head with distinct eyes, and some sort of drive slot that could pass for a mouth. "The company would please me. Greetings, Bart."

Bart shuffled a little, trying to work this out. Old had said their names were too complicated for human folk, but certainly there was something they could do. "Is there something I can call you?"

"I will adopt a human name for your ease. Call me Chad."

"Oh, no," Bart said. "I don't want to call you a human name. I'd like to call you what you prefer."

"I prefer Chad. It is a casual-sounding name that respects social boundaries while implying a counter-culture longing. I have always wanted someone to call me this."

"Ok. Well, Chad, do you mind me asking something else." Bart tapped their pronoun pin. "Is there an etiquette to pronoun use for robots?" Bart really hoped they'd asked that a polite way, but they knew if someone had a question for them, they'd prefer they asked it rather than continuing to do something Bart didn't like.

Chad's head swiveled over. "Our gender is indicated by a matrix of light hues on our shoulder. While some have other preferences, it is custom to default to xe ... around these parts." Chad seemed disappointed when Bart was still thinking how to respond. "I have incorporated human idiom gleaned from your speech patterns. I was trying to gift you with humor. If I've offended, I apologize."

"No, no, Chad, that was great. I 'spose it might help to remember that my brain doesn't go as fast as your circuits. Besides that, I'm trying to make sure I don't offend. I'm new here."

"I like you, Bart, and my probability reading indicates we will get along fine. I have only minimal shades of gender, since I postulate you do not know that is what these lights indicate." Xe pointed to a dim pattern of light on xyr shoulder. "Your bottle is watching me."

Bart looked over, surprised. It wasn't always clear who could and couldn't see the stout bottle, with its fancy torn label.

"Robots know a lot, Bart," Old whispered. Then, louder, "Hi, Chad. I'm Old. I'm Bart's whiskey bottle. So we were hoping to get me filled up here. Any recommendations?"

"Bart swept the manure today with excellent enthusiasm and my tracks kept more clean than normal so I will purchase for you any drinks that you both consume." Chad's voice was a bit louder than Bart was hoping for on that one. "Furthermore, to save you the awkward choice of imbibing unpleasant whiskey in order to minimize spending of my credits, I will select choices for you both, with your permission."

"Sounds good!" Old said with a marker-face grin. Now, hold up, Bart hadn't really—

Aww, turns out Chad was waiting for Bart's consent too. "As long as it's not a hardship, Chad, I'd appreciate your recommendation and kindness." Bart didn't know if Chad had regular work, but when a folk had to find jobs like scrapin' shit every day for a living, they sure did appreciate when a folk bought them a drink.

Bart did have a moment of remembering Chad was solo-drinking a margarita pitcher and Bart didn't care for sweet drinks, but they needn't have worried. Old disappeared for a minute or two, and returned beaming from horizon to horizon, filled with a deep amber liquid. And as Bart reached out, they were surprised to see they'd been served something too. And it was blue.

"Chad, is this going to alter me in any ways I might regret?" They didn't want to be rude, but a folk had the right to know what they were putting in their body.

"No, I made sure the bartender knew you were a pure-bred. I selected this drink based on my scan of you and your likely preferences. I'll tell you what's in it if you'd like, but if you'll trust me, it might be more fun to give it a try."

Bart wasn't letting all that go but it didn't seem the right time to pick at it, either. Chad's lights blinked on and off in a regular rhythm. You know, they did trust xem. Bart leaned in and sniffed it, expecting something too sweet or maybe even a Curaçao. Instead of citrus, there was almost a scent of pine. Of moss. Like the forest. And as they leaned over further, a slight mist rose up over the top of the lowball, like the morning haze over a quiet lake when a folk just wanted a moment to themself. They took a sip.

"Dang, Chad, this is one of the most interesting things I've ever had."

"Sometimes humans use interesting to avoid saying they didn't like something. Is that the situation here?"

Itchy britches, robots could be passive aggressive. "Not in this case, Chad. I said interesting because I've never had anything like it. I also really enjoy it. Thank you so much."

Bart was kinda glad Chad had offered to buy the thing. Given how much everything had cost at the horse gift shop, who knows what smokin' forest drinks went for here.

The robot with the pink drink swiveled around. "Greetings. Did I hear we have a purebred visitor?"

"Now, look, I am not comfortable—"

"Their name is Bart," Chad answered. "We are friends. You were not invited to interrupt."

"Oh, it's alright, Chad." Bart liked Chad just fine, but they had to set some boundaries. "I'm Bart, like Chad said. Is there something I can call you?"

Bart couldn't help but cover their ears at whatever screech came out of the bot's speakers.

"They cannot vocalize ##...---,!," Chad shouted. "You have performed a rude action!"

"Chad, now, I appreciate you, but I can handle myself."

Old peered at Bart nervously, but Bart gave it a reassuring nod. Bart could take care of themself, as long as this didn't go all dystopian on them.

"I do not use human names. You may refer to me as

Robot and she. I am sorry that my name offended you. We can sing popular music together," she added. "We have data from all human eras and can sing poorly for others' amusement."

Bart had enough to unpack for the time. "Oh, we'll see about the singing, but may I ask what you're drinking? It looks good."

"Everclear and strawberries."

Grandfather's Lord Almighty. "Oh, alright."

"So, bantering, what has brought you to our town today?" Chad interrupted.

"My friend Horse had a dentist appointment, and she's part of my posse so we stick together."

"You know how far in advance you have to make those," Robot said.

"Yep, well it's been nice today," Bart said, fidgeting.

A passing robot piped up behind them. "It's 298 degrees today, with partial clouds and no chance of rain."

Chad turned to the bot. "This is my friend. We are conversing."

A flying robot hovered near, its fans blowing in Bart's face. "Are you finding it difficult to communicate with us? We know that we are advanced."

Bart lifted their hands, hoping the bots would back off and give them a little more personal space. They didn't. "I am not trying to be rude here—" Bart meant that but was losing their patience, "—but isn't this Future Town? Like I'm not even going ta' ask if I've actually time traveled to this place, but whatever that means, wouldn't robots have learned human behavior a little more by now?"

The robots all around quieted. Bart heard a slow whirr and several *bweeeyoup* type noises. "We live only with horses. Training to human behavior is done from select human data."

"I have not trained recently," Robot admitted, her hydraulics lowering some.

"I have been on WoW," Chad said. "Mechagon is hilarious."

"It is offensive!" another robot called out.

"You're offensive!" Chad responded. "You carry your oil in a clear canister!"

Bart stood up, though not before being sure to finish the rest of that blue drink. "I stopped by for a bit of cheer and maybe to meet a friend. I'm not looking to stir any folk up. Maybe I need to go."

The bartender slid down a long track, blowing a long silver horn. Bart couldn't hear any sound from it, but the whole placed quieted right down.

"We request you stay with us," xe said. "We will adjust to your social needs. What can I get you? We stock all beverages and have printing capability for any vessels or accessories you may require. All further drinks are complimentary for your trouble."

Chad seemed to be saying something in robot-speak to the bartender, but Bart was thinking about what xe'd said. *Printing?* Like 3-D printing? Must be, if they could make accessories. Bart was pretty sure these folk didn't have a finesse for origami.

"I'd just like a whiskey. Not the worst stuff," they amended. "But something friendly. And, with your printers, how much would you charge to make something that looked like this?" Glad to see there was a napkin, Bart scratched out a sketch and some dimensions and handed it over.

"There is no charge. I insist. This is for a horse?"

Bart tried not to let their face look too sappy. "It sure is. A real good friend."

"Then we will print it with platinum and polish it. Horse friend, Horse, will like." The bartender looked at the counter. "Would you like your whiskey now, human barfriend?"

"Er . . ." Bart gathered themself. "Yes. Yes, I sure would."

And after hearing about Chad's dreams of visiting a human city, and Robot's favorite Taylor Swift songs, and meeting about two dozen other robots and finally telling the bartender, who liked to be called Ice, that it was time for them to go, Bart left.

They didn't notice Old had been refilled again until they left, and noticed it swaying a little, side to side. Only then did Bart realize this town probably didn't even have an inn. That was fine. They'd slept outside many a'time.

A whirr sounded behind them. It was Robot.

"Hey. I've got some friends who have a human sleeping room. They will likely be nosy after you awake and ask about human life but they will not take your small amount of coins. Are you interested in staying with them?"

Bart paused a moment, not wanting to embarrass themself with a hiccup. "Sure, Robot. That'd be swell."

They did glance around real quick to see if Horse was around, but not recognizing her among the late-night crowds of horses and robots, they stumbled back. And went to sleep. With real nice dreams of quiet lakes and deep skies.

Just Bart: Episode 14

Human Life

"In which Bart questions humanity too ... "

Bart couldn't move. They panicked a moment, feeling around and realizing they were tightly tucked into soft sheets with a flannel cover. Like, tightly tucked in. And what was— Bart pulled a little stuffed bear out from under their arm. Now, that was cute ... maybe. Dependin' on where they were.

Grunting, they wriggled out of the tight covers, trying to remember what had happened. Where was the posse?

Old was laying on the foot of the bed, still asleep by its lack of little marker face, but they didn't see Tom or Horse. Or, er, Twinkle.

Oh, right Future Town. Lived in by Horses and Robots. They'd gone to the robot bar with Old, and someone had offered them a free place to sleep. Something like that. At least that fancy robot drink had them sleeping nicely for once. And the bed seemed caring, if not all a bit creepy. Well, in a spot of trouble, it sure was nice to have folk look after you.

Bart stretched, sitting up. *Hell!*

Turned out about thirty robots were lined up, staring at them. They were going to call it staring, anyway. Some had eyes that were more in eye-places than others, but the point was they were definitely being fixed upon.

"Good morning, Bart," they said in unison. Then, one of the robots beeped. Yeah, Bart had worked with that sort.

"Good morning, er, folk. I do appreciate being offered a bed to sleep on. I suppose I'll be moving along now."

The robots all spoke at once. "We have voted on a communal name for your ease of use. We should be called Banjoko. We have many questions for you."

"Now, hold up." Bart rubbed their head. "I haven't even had coffee."

A cranking noise sounded, and the robots hastened to part as a tank pulled forward, with a spout protruding from the middle. A coffee cup swung on a wire holder. A little uneasy but not wanting to be rude, Bart poured a cup, surprised to see it steaming and emitting a real welcoming smell. They did prefer a dark roast. "Thanks!" Bart said.

"You are welcome," the tank answered, two flaps opening to reveal eyes. Bart clamped their fingers to avoid dropping the cup. "At least no one can see this," Bart murmured to themself.

"We are all recording you," Banjoko said.

"Okaaay," Bart said, at this point just drinking the coffee and hoping to leave. It was good coffee.

"Do not worry. We value human consent in Future Town. We are not like humans. You are not streaming."

This was officially irritating. Bart had issues with human folk too, but they didn't need to hear about it from a bunch of robots.

"Except in universes where streaming is mandatory," one corrected.

"We have some questions for you, if you will consent," the group said. "It would be appreciated. Unrelated, we hope you enjoyed your sleep here."

Dang passive aggressive robots. Fine, a couple of questions couldn't hurt. Being practical, Bart had just had a long, no-cost sleep after a night at the robot bar. "Alright, I suppose I can answer a question or two. Is there a bathroom I could use?"

A panel in the floor opened, and a bowl-like device rose from it, along with a strong scent of . . . fabric detergent?

"We have plumbing and sanitation."

With a grimace, Bart looked at the toilet. "Can I ask if this one is . . . sentient?"

The robots all laughed, a percussive, metallic laugh. "It is not a robot. It is a toilet."

"Well, wait, what about the coffee maker?"

Several robots clicked and beeped as if Bart had offended. This would need to be unpacked later. But right now, Bart did have to go.

They sighed. "I apologize for any offense. I'm human, so I don't understand all of this." That seemed to appease them. "Now, look, where I'm from we don't like folk watching. Can you look away? Cameras too. Turn it all that way." They waved. After a series of beeps, they at least saw a few shutters close. That would have to do.

The toilet, or urinal, or whatever it was had a little sink on top, and after Bart washed their hands, the whole apparatus lowered back into the floor. Bart had been thinking about asking for a shower, but that was settled now.

"Alright. All set there. So, you had a question?"

"Multiple questions. Here is the first. Humans glorify violence in the context of a chain of dominance throughout organic beings evolved from the same chain. Yet human societies achieve enlightenment once humanity separates itself as a non-perpetuator of violence, lowering itself back down the chain it just climbed to instead serve as its protector. Can you explain the tipping point in the human psyche related to violence and its employment as part of the human experience."

"*Lawrence Welk marathon*, guys. I haven't even finished the coffee yet. Can you take the questions down a notch?"

After a series of clicking sounds, another tried again.

"Cats are violent carnivores with piercing teeth and questionable hygiene. Why are they symbolic of comfort?"

"I don't know." Was this a trick question? "They're soft and rumbly and make us feel tough like we live with tiny lions. Can we go a little lighter? Warm this up a little more?"

Clicking sounds. "We wish to know what you find more satisfying. Spreading creamed animal excretions onto cakes and scraping them flat with a knife, pouring resin over broken wood and then sanding it a dozen different ways, or cooking impractically tiny food in a doll-size kitchen."

"What?" Bart didn't watch any of that. An occasional *Toot and Boot*, sure. Raja was the damn coolest human since Prince. But maybe they didn't need to mention that to the robots. "How is this the question you have for all of humanity?"

"We as robots remain highly intrigued by satisfying

videos displayed on the human AI hive mind. Our algorithms show that satisfying videos would show the reparation of climate damage caused by humanity or new alliances for world peace, but monetization peaks for congealed cow-fluid baked inside of pre-made dough and then cut open."

Bart shifted the hat on their head. "Well, what do you watch? What videos are satisfying to robots?"

The room grew completely silent.

"Next question for you as human. We have watched *Who's the Boss?* in its entirety in multiple universes and the question is not clearly resolved."

Finally, something Bart could answer. "It's Mona. Her sexual liberation from traditional age and gender roles served as a pointed contrast to the satirical juxtaposition of the presumed leads. That made Mona the boss."

Banjoko clattered loudly at this, and Bart had a sense they were voting over what to ask them next. "Ask about ALF," one said. "He remains confusing."

This was starting to feel like trivia night, and Bart was not a fan. How was anyone supposed to talk with that voice booming out? Maybe the robots could answer *that*. "Hey," they said instead, "don't you have all of human history in a database? In multiple universes, sounds like. Can't you get at your training data?"

The buzz intensified. "This is such a finite way of thinking," a robot responded. "Each human is unique. Are you nothing more than your history?"

Bart did not have a robot brain, so they had to think what Banjoko was gettin' at here. Yeah, they supposed, they sure hoped they brought something new to the stew. "So you've asked like a billion humans these questions, and like all of our grandparents . . . but now you want *my* take?"

"Yes," dozens of vocal processors answered at once.

"My grandunits were brandist," one robot muttered.

Bart sighed, looking at the robot who'd spoken. "You can't take on the guilt of your previous model years; you can only use their lessons to acknowledge and help dismantle any remaining structural brandism."

"I'm not bad?" the robot asked.

"What? I hope not. Now, I've much appreciated your hospitality, but I need to be going."

"Another question!" The robots nearly shouted in unison.

"Alright, sure, one more. Make it a good one."

"In your human politics"—

Uh, oh.

—"why is it that the judgment of an act depends on the organizational affiliation of the actor?"

Bart didn't need to get into this. As if Angel's mom getting social media hadn't been enough of a challenge. "Search for hypocrisy. Then emotional labor. Hey, look, I'm happy to help, but I've got a friend in town, and I ought to be on my way."

A unit nearly squealed out, "They are trying to leave! Ask them something less offensive!"

"Will you be watching *Picard*?"

Will I be watching Picard? Bart sat back down on the bed, and pulled the little bear into their arms.

"*Picard* is a validation of everything we were and everything we've become. It acknowledges the pain, the loss, and now the impending *arrival* of its namesake generation, and will do so with the same subtlety and universality of its original, well I mean not original, but originating series."

Bart raised a silencing hand to the stirring robots.

"So here's the thing about *The Next Generation*. That wasn't just a show. And those weren't just actors doin' it. The depth of those characters was only surpassed by the naked vulnerability of the ties between them. Through their differences as well as their common yearning for freedom, they showed us what it meant to be *alive*." Bart took a breath.

"What about in Season Two when—"

NEIGH!

Bart jumped up from the bed, setting down the bear. *Dang, what was I doing?*

Banjoko shook at the sound outside, communicating from what Bart could tell in immediate robot speak, amongst their, like, networks or whatever.

"It's Horse!" one said.

Bart had learned that every horse in Future Town went by Horse, but they also knew that voice. Unable to prevent a big, beaming smile, they stood. "I am so grateful for your hospitality, but as you could hear, it's time for me to go. Now, jolan tru, friends."

The robots continued to chatter, flash, and beep as Bart picked up Old, grabbed their things, put on their pineapple leather boots, and walked through a hallway and out onto the street. Another human was walking by, scooping horse shit from the road. "Howdy," Bart said.

"Howdy," the folk returned with a tip of the hat.

And there was Horse, along with Tom, who was glowing brightly again. At their sight, Old wriggled from Bart's grasp and flew into the air.

Soon Twinkle was there too. She smacked Old in the side. "Settle down, Bart, that's our high five."

Hmm. Bart turned toward Horse. "Hey, Horse! How are your teeth?"

Horse neighed up again at the building where Bart had slept. Now that they could see it in the daylight, it looked like one of those storage container buildings.

"Look, I went to a robot bar, and—"

Neigh!

"She says just stop," Old said. "Her teeth are great. She wants to show you something."

Horse opened her lips, and Bart was surprised to see a huge sapphire, nestled onto some sort of tooth cover.

"It's a grill," Old said. "She wants to know if you like it."

"Sure do," Bart said. But suddenly the things they'd got Horse, as top notch as they were, didn't seem quite as good. Old was staring at them funny. "Just seems like the stuff we got might not measure up."

Horse walked up and nudged Bart's arm. Bart reached into their messenger bag.

"Well, first they call this unicorn hair." They showed Horse the rainbow clip of hair and with her nod, secured it into her tail. Horse swished her tail around, happily, the rainbow strands bouncing with it. "And then this." They held up the wide silver chain from the robot bar, sized to fit around Horse's ears but not interfere with her tiara. In huge, expertly printed and polished, platinum letters, it said: HORSE.

Horse whinnied, more gently this time.

"Bart," Twinkle said, as Horse bent down so Bart could put the chain on her. "Horse says those are the sweetest, most thoughtful gifts a horse could ever receive. And she knows Future Town's real expensive, so you either had to sacrifice your dignity or—" Bart narrowed their eyes. "Even if you'd cut that from scrap paper, Horse would think it was a treasure for the Horse Queen."

"Sometimes," Bart said, lowering their voice. "I think you're the Horse Queen."

"Saying that could get you a quarter in horse jail," Twinkle whispered. As Bart's head jerked up, Horse whinnied and Twinkle raised a hand. "It's a joke! There's no horse jail; do you think horses are assholes?"

Bart grimaced. "Well, then, would it be fine if we could move along from this place?"

"Sure thing, Bart." Tom answered, this time. "How are your coins?"

A little embarrassed, Bart didn't want to admit how much they'd spent on Horse's unicorn hair. It sure looked pretty on her. "They're fine. Just fine. Just . . . I'll need to get some work at the next town."

Feeling the nearly empty bag that was tied to their belt,

they looked again at Horse, who was tossing her tail again, the rainbow threads sparkling in the sunlight.

It was worth it.

Just Bart: Episode 15

Secret Santa

"An exchange of gifts ..."

Bart whistled as they measured the angle and whisked the chalk along the square. They turned to pick up the saw, then jolted as they saw Old floating before them.

Old wasn't supposed to be here while Bart was working. But it was still full, and swayed a little in the air, like a person might with their hands in their pockets.

"Hey, Old. I thought you were getting some rest today."

"I was," it said, its little marker eyes darting off to the side. "But I got to thinking, it's the holidays again. And you're here, working, like you always are. I'd like us to take a break. For the holidays."

Old knew that a folk can't always take a break when there's coins needed. But they'd got a solid day in here, so maybe a couple hours tonight could work.

"Everyone deserves a break for the holidays," Old had continued.

"They don't always get it," Bart couldn't help but say.

"I know, Bart, but they should."

"Yeah." Bart looked down and sawed the next segment. Pulling the coarse sandpaper from where they'd tucked it, they glanced back over to Old. "Yeah. Is after I'm done fine with you?"

"Sure, Bart, that would be great."

Bart stopped. "Hold on, though. How is it already the holidays?" Old didn't answer, so they scratched their head, that itchy spot on the side of their hat.

"I don't really worry about it," Old said, its mouth forming a tiny line. "Maybe there was some time dilation from going to EarthCon after all. That can happen."

"Oh." Bart held the piece up into the window opening. A little putty for that old damage and that would work fine. "But . . . does that mean EarthCon is coming up again?"

"Maybe," Old said, tilting some. "Anyway, we've all been working on something. Something fun!"

Bart set down the piece of frame. "Alright, what is it?"

Now, Old didn't have hands, but as if it did, a heavy looking crystal dish appeared in front of it full of paper scraps. "Old, is that an ash tray?"

Old angled forward, its face disappearing for a moment.

Bart never knew how these things worked. Was the ash tray magic too? Bart wasn't one for smoking, but they wanted to be polite. "So, then, is it . . . alive . . . like you?"

"No, Bart, no," Old said, its eyes making little hollow circles. "It passed away."

Bart stepped back, stumbling out an apology.

"Oh, come on, Bart, you're always in the weeds. Do you want to do Secret Santa or not?"

Miss Kitty. "It does not sound appealing at this juncture, no," they said, mostly staring at that ash tray.

"Come on, Bart, we all just give one of us a gift, so

everyone gets one. But you have to pick a piece of paper. And don't say!"

"Is my name in there?"

Old's face contracted. "Pick. A. Paper."

"Alright." Bart rustled around but not *too long* and came up with a little strip. "Oh, I—"

"No talking about it!" The ash tray disappeared and Bart would'a thought they'd imagined it, but the little paper was still in their hand.

"I'll see you back at the inn after I'm done and paid up?"

"Sounds good, Bart." Old wiggled. "It's going to be fun."

Bart tipped their hat. "I'll see you later."

Feeling a little warmer inside, Bart stared a moment at that strip of paper. This was not going to be easy. Giving a gift was a special way to show love. Bart wanted to do it right. And this was not something they were so great at.

Fortunately, they had the whole rest of the afternoon to think about it, along with some fine woodwork that ended up fitting just right, if Bart did say so.

Bart walked back to the market in the dark, well, it was getting dark real early, with a reasonable amount of coins. Jingling them in their hand, they worried. This was a small town, and gifts should be special. They walked down the street, tapping their chin. If only they had more time.

And that's when they figured it out.

When they wound back around to the inn, Horse was waiting right out front. Tom, glowing brightly, was swirling around her, along with Old and Twinkle, the sprite of ambiguous autonomy their friend MageBoss had conjured for Horse.

Bart was ready for the plumbed water closet and a fresh bar of that charcoal soap. Then they saw their travel bag sitting at Horse's hooves.

"Yeah," Old said. "Turns out they don't care for horses and ghosts in this place, but we're fine—Tom talked to the team and set us up."

But magic bottles were ok? And what team? Then Bart remembered how many scraps of paper were in the, er, dish.

Horse whinnied gently, her tiara and forehead chain glinting in the lamplight, and then a glowing light grew on the dusty street. Now, Bart had seen one'a Horse's holiday portals before, and they noticed that the whole group did glance around a bit.

"Come on!" Twinkle said, glittering into view. The sprite stuck her hip out to one side and made a face, before darting through the portal.

With a shrug, Horse followed through, Tom close behind.

Hefting up their bag, Bart looked at Old. "Guess that's it then."

Not totally ready for another horse world just yet, Bart was real relieved when they stepped into a nice, wizardy, tavern of sorts. Just the genre Bart liked, it had a olde-thyme vibe like a fantasy inn but the cleanliness of a fancy sorcery hall. No musty smells or raucous assaults, the place looked . . . well, like a rental.

Bart glanced up over the door, where one arrow pointed to **Rystrooms** and other large, wooden sign said in jolly, weathered paint: **The Merlin Room.**

Speaking of wizards, Bart was glad to see the two folk waiting around a tall table. Sal held up a bright red goblet, tiny bells jingling around her hefty arm. She wore a right pretty black lace cape, hooked in the middle across a low-cut red velvet dress, as always so her EPIC chest tattoo was framed over a necklace of gears and red glass. Instead of a fascinator this time, she had bright red, cropped hair with a couple black pins sticking from the strands.

See, Bart was simple and not much one for fashion, but Sal looked terrific. And next to her, MageBoss had dressed for the occasion as well. The first time they'd met per, per'd just had a' old gray wizard robe on. Per'd dressed up fancy for the game night, but this time per was dressed for holiday cheer, with a gold robe so shiny Bart could hardly see whatever else per was wearing.

"Happy Holidays!" Bart said. They looked down at their own simple clothes, covered in a bit of sawdust from setting window frames all day. They glanced over at Old who seemed to be reading their mind.

"It's ok," Old said. "They like you as you. You know these two; they love dressing up."

Well, at least Bart had their pineapple leather boots. Those sure were fine. They stepped back a bit, makin' sure they were visible.

"Hello, Bart!" Sal smiled warmly, and MageBoss nodded next to her.

"It's a rental, but don't worry, I know some pers. No charge."

Well, that was right nice. MageBoss knew everyone, it seemed.

"You ready for Secret Santa?" Sal asked.

Bart did sorta' cringe. They'd never personally been a Santa sort—the whole thing got real weird even without the problematic—but they knew you can't say that to folk because people are dang serious about Santa.

"Something wrong?" Twinkle bubbled, zipping around.

Well if a sprite's gonna call you out.

"Oh, I'm real excited, and yes I'm ready. Was just musin' whether we could have a more inclusive name."

"What do you want to call it, Secret Dan?" Tom snorted, glowing suddenly next to them.

"Horse says they call it Snooping Horse," Old added.

After a brief silence, Sal swung forward her glass. "There's drinks at the bar. Mulled wine, cranberry juice, water, fresh lemon, and gin."

"What are you drinking, Sal?" Tom asked.

"A cocktail."

Well, Bart did figure you could do something with all that. Thing is, they didn't hear whiskey, and they did notice a slight look of worry on Old's face. Old had said this was just for the evenin'. Bart would make sure it was taken care of when they got back.

A few minutes later, everyone had moved to a nice cozy round couch, surrounding a low stone table. Sal was lounged out with one arm across the back and the other on her goblet,

MageBoss was sitting with a less stressed out smile than Bart had seen on per, and Bart just hoped they didn't leave a sawdust butt mark on the couch. That was really it for the seating. Horse stood by them with Twinkle darting around, and Tom and Old wove around a crystal chandelier like they were playing a game.

"Horse, I'm sorry," MageBoss said, "the rental team didn't know what to do for horse seating."

Horse raised her head.

"This is horse seating," Old said. "But why doesn't she open her gift first?"

Horse nudged Old's glass body with her nose, but it seemed friendly enough.

"Alright. Who had a gift for Horse?" MageBoss said.

Bart supposed it wasn't per.

Sal sat up, setting the goblet down on a lace coaster she seemed to have pulled from a pocket. Also, she pulled out a shiny piece of lavender fabric, tied with a little cream ribbon and decorated with a sprig of something purple. Well, Bart supposed, probably lavender. Yeah, they could smell that soap smell from here.

"She asks if you'll open it," Twinkle said.

"Sure thing, pal."

Horse tapped a little on the ground as Sal slid the little ribbon off, revealing a rose-colored piece of lace with black ribbons through it. Bart had no idea what it was.

"A tail tutu!" Twinkle said, rushing over. "She's always wanted one!"

There was just too much in the world that Bart didn't know.

Yet Horse seemed right happy as Sal got up and tied the little lace at the top of Horse's tail, where it puffed up, well, a lot like a tutu. Bart smiled as they saw the unicorn hair woven into her tail. It did look good, but Horse sure liked that tutu.

"I'll go next!" Twinkle said, and for a moment there, Bart wasn't sure if this was the sprite, or the sprite talkin' for the horse. It all got confusing at times. But then Twinkle said, "This gift is for you, Old!"

Now, if the sprite wasn't real, how was she included in the gift exchange? Old cut Bart a glance that read real clear like "don't take this away from me" and Bart sat back and canned it as Twinkle suddenly burst a giant spray of glitter out onto the table and everyone squealed in delight.

Prince's Pager. Bart started to cover their nose, but then the glitter disappeared just as quickly. What was left on the table was a huge decanter of amber liquid and a simple, not fancy lowball.

"Oooh!" Old exclaimed. And without Bart even touching a thing, the decanter filled Old up to the top and filled the glass just the level Bart liked it.

The bottle spun around, its torn little label almost glowing. "Thanks, Twinkle! You're the best!"

But I thought— Well, Bart wasn't going to mess with any holiday spirit. He took a sip from the glass. Oh, it was the *good* stuff.

"And what did I get?" Twinkle asked.

MageBoss casually pulled a wand from per side, and flicked a wrist, causing a second sprite to appear next to Twinkle.

Bart took a little more of that whiskey.

"I've got something for you, MageBoss," Tom said. "Horse?" Now, Bart did not know how Horse was carrying such a thing, but suddenly a molded figurine appeared on the table. One of those "sexy" figurines from one of the new games.

"Eluph," MageBoss whispered, carrying the thing like a baby and wrapping it into some bubble wrap that had just appeared. "This'll go on my best shelf! Thanks, man."

Then what looked like a plastic horse to Bart but Sal hailed as a My Little Horse Classic appeared on the table. She leapt up, hugging Horse, who looked pretty darn happy as they almost rocked back and forth.

"Bart?" MageBoss asked. "Who did you have?"

Bart looked down at the strips of paper in their hand. They didn't know if they measured up. Tom didn't really have hands, so slowly, they held up the paper. "Tom, well, these are for you."

Tom floated over, flickering a little. His ghosty face peered in, and his mouth seemed to be reading the text to himself. "Really, Bart? Will . . . will you go with me?"

"Sure, Tom."

Tom spun around to the others. "There's a lumberjack competition in town. Bart got us two tickets. There's log rolling, and sculpting. Gee, thanks, Bart. We'll have a good time."

Bart knew that Tom, as a ghost, could have just gone. Tom had his things, but he was ethical. And Bart knew he wouldn't go alone. "I'll hold onto 'm," Bart muttered, putting the tickets in a pocket.

Well, they supposed that was it. They leaned back with another sip of that whiskey.

"Bart," Sal said. "What did you get?"

Bart already had everything they needed. They weren't sure how to say that. But who was left?

Old drifted over, a shy look on its face. "Bart, I don't have much for ya'."

"It's fine, Old, you and I have been through a lot."

"Sure," Old said, its eyes quivering. "But I still got you what I could. It's a song."

Old started to sing, a nice song, a song that you know and love. And Bart sang along, and Horse and her sprite and her sprite, and Sal and MageBoss, and Tom too, glowing along with all the pretty lights.

Bart sipped from their glass and sang that song. And Bart hoped that everyone out there would have a nice holiday.

Maybe next year, they thought, maybe next year some things can be different. Bart wasn't ready to think about all of it, but then decided maybe thinking it at all is enough for now.

Eventually, when the lights had dimmed and the mulled wine was empty and Horse made a new portal, Bart stepped through.

Happy Holidays.

Just Bart: Episode 16

Funky Portal

"2020 was supposed to be normal . . ."

A truly lovely holiday party behind them, Bart stepped through the portal Horse made.

Ah!

Bart's arms flailed for something to grab but there was nothing there. Blackness, the stars, and the posse. Like, not even a ground. Somehow, Bart, Tom, Old, Horse, and the sprites were floating in space.

Horse hiccupped.

"Ok, so here is the situation," Old said. "Horse had a lot of holiday cheer at the party."

Bart raised an eyebrow.

"Gin," Tom elaborated. "Horse is lit."

"What?" Bart wasn't trying to shame any . . . horse, but was that . . . appropriate? More relevantly, was it safe to float in space? "Can we even breathe out here?"

"What kind of story do you think this is?" Old asked.

"Yeah, we'd already have exploded," Tom agreed. "I think we're in a bubble." Tom's ghosty face scrunched, and he glanced at Old. "I don't want to hear it."

"Ok, so we've ported to the middle of space. Before I ask any more obvious questions, is this, you know, at least our neighborhood? I'd love to see Jupiter."

Tom glowed. "I'd love to see—"

Bart cut him off with a sharp glare.

"Actually, no," the second sprite said.

Bart wasn't even sure if this new sprite had a name, or if they were also considered Horse's sprite, or Twinkle's sprite. Maybe they didn't want to know all of it. Bart rubbed their forehead.

"We're so far away from Earth your mind could not comprehend it," the sprite continued.

Bart's mind had come to comprehend a lot. But they had better things to worry about than condescending sprites. "Alright. And, uh, can I call you something?"

"Yes! I'm Sparkle. She/they." She did a little backflip in the air, with silver glitter trailing in her wake.

Oh, maybe Sparkle was alright. "I'm Bart." They tapped their brassy pronoun pin. "They/them."

"Can we focus on the fact that we are suspended in Sector 7 space?" Tom seemed worried.

Bart squinted. "If we're only in Sector 7, how far away can that be? I figured it'd be like Sector Quizzajillion or something." No one reacted. "Well, hell, at least we didn't port into EarthCon."

Old glanced away uneasily.

"So, uh." Bart looked at Horse. She seemed to be concentrating.

A glow of light expanded to the side, and while Bart was glad not to be stranded in space for eternity with a ghost, a horse, a whiskey bottle, and two sprites, they suddenly realized this slice of Sector 7 was likely a place no Earth person had seen, maybe no being at all. They gazed out one long moment into the indigo-washed, light-spattered background of eternity. And stepped through.

There was a ground this time. But it was not Earth.

Bart was surrounded by a sea of … tiny people? Tiny naked people? Bart had no idea. The little gray figures started running up their body and around their arms. Afraid to move, Bart stared in panic at Horse.

"Oops. This is definitely Goblinland," Old said, turning back and forth like it was shaking a head in disbelief. "Horse must be *real* wasted to reach Goblinland. It is hard to get to. Like, *legendary* hard."

Horse neighed softly.

Tom opened and closed his mouth a few times, as though suspicious of something. Then he closed it.

"Yeah, that's fine," Bart said. "Goblinland, sure. They seem great. Can we get out of here? I'm not looking to hurt any little buddies, and they are mighty small." One of the goblins reached Bart's hand, staring up at them with wide eyes. They opened their mouth and sharp, pointy teeth sparkled in the violet light.

The goblin lifted their arms and began to sing. Not just sing, but sing one of those 1960's holiday songs that was just weird by today's standard but no one wanted to take the social media avalanche for just sayin' the thing was ready to retire.

Besides, it was January now!

Then the other goblins all joined in, joyfully pronouncing a bunch of rhymey slang that probably wasn't even used then.

"Alright, friends. Thanks for that, but we need to be on our way."

They did not stop singing. Horse had closed her eyes like she had a headache. Tom was turned away and Old had hidden itself into Bart's messenger bag. Bart glanced desperately at the sprites. "Twinkle, Sparkle, you know the deal here?"

"Yeah, goblins read your minds for what songs they think you like the most. Except it's *not* what you like, it's what's the most invasive, since that's been dragged over your brain cells over and over."

Dragged over my what?

Bart didn't like this. Luckily, they'd just come from a holiday party because otherwise the whole world would be singing one of those car company commercial songs with nonsense lyrics that sound vaguely emotional. "What about Horse?" they asked over the chorus. "Can she make a portal?"

"No! She's getting a huge headache and the songs are too distracting."

"Well, we can't just stay here!" Panicking, Bart realized the goblins had switched to one of those storytelling Santa songs. At least it wasn't one of the sexual innuendo songs. Yet.

"We gotta counter it with something." Bart adjusted their hat, tryin'ta think.

"Like a better holiday song?" Old asked, its bottle cap peeking just out of Bart's bag. "The Dramatics or the Whispers or something?"

"No," Sparkle answered. "We've got to think of

something so startling it makes them all pause long enough for Horse to make a portal. They're mind readers, so don't say it. Just think it real hard. A big song. Epic."

Tom glowed brightly, and both sprites zipped around, but nothing happened. Horse still had her eyes closed and Old was back in the bag. Ok. Bart could do this. Songs. So many songs. Jingles, and holiday staples, and dance trends, and songs that people love and still hope no one notices how problematic they are. Songs about havin' bass, and callin' people, and yeah mostly just more innuendos. Heck, Bart couldn't unremember half the stuff they heard when they were young, like that time that their grandparents were singing and dancing to that song by the B-52's guy about the monster in his pants and it was literally just about—

The goblins were staring at them. A circle of light shot out, and all the goblins climbing on Bart hopped off. "Bye, remember, it's January now," Bart called and hurried through.

Guardian Angel Prince! Bart closed their eyes for a moment, hoping wherever they were, it was just a simple road through a simple town, with simple folk like Bart, and simple work so Bart could earn some coin, and make sure this was a regular, normal, year.

It looked like a Taco Bell. Sort of. It was a big room, with no tables or chairs, just ledges around three sides of the room and a big counter at the other. Horse had stumbled up to the front.

Tom floated back, forming into a dispassionate shrug. "She's hungry. You want anything?"

"Yes. I would like to return to my life."

Everyone got real quiet.

"Here, just get me a taco." They looked at the board. "Oat meat. With avocado. I'll put on my own hot sauce."

Bart couldn't help but notice that the other horses were watching them with amusement as they used their fingers to help eat. "Speciesist horses," they muttered.

"Sorry about that," Sparkle said. "Horses can be really uncouth after holiday parties."

Bart *almost* asked where they were. They didn't feel it was regular Earth, but if it was Future Town again, it might be best to move along without knowing.

"Where is she?" Bart asked, not seeing Horse. Or the sprites for that matter.

"Bathroom, Bart." Tom rolled his eyes.

A minute later, a portal formed in the middle of the restaurant.

Bart walked over to Horse and leaned in. "You alright? If we need to rest somewhere, we can."

Horse rested her nose on Bart's shoulder. Then stepped through.

The next place was some sort of horse porno thing. Horse neighed loudly and Tom stared, and Bart did not hesitate when that next portal appeared.

"Horse!" Bart's eyes were probably still wide. "Look, we ought to be getting home. If you need help, we can help you. Otherwise, can ya concentrate this time? On getting *home?* Specifically?"

Solemnly, Horse nodded.

Tom was still staring back from where they'd just emerged, but one of the sprites spoke up. Oh, it was Twinkle.

"We're sorry. We're trying."

"It's ok, Horse." Bart looked around, a bit nervously. To their surprise, they were standing in what appeared to be a museum. White walls, white floors, and sparsely displayed pieces. Nothing too exciting, from what Bart could see. Still life paintings of apples in baskets and such. Soft classical music wafted through the spacious hall.

Old was peeking out of Bart's bag, a skeptical tilt to its marker-drawn face. They exchanged a glance.

Twinkle spun in place. "This time, I think we can do it. We'll just concentrate." As if assisting in that concentration, Sparkle and Twinkle began to hum in harmonious tones. Bart felt a sense of peace. This was alright. This would get them home.

The portal glowed with extra resolve, and Bart walked through, eyes wide open to see—

"Oops," Sparkle said.

They appeared to be in Angel's living room. Her parents were there, and her siblings, all gathered on the couches as if enjoying a game.

This was damn embarrassing.

Angel's mom broke into a huge smile, and her little brother started to walk over, a defiant look on his face. Everyone else was pretty much staring.

Angel stood up. She had on a football jersey and a slack pair of jeans. Her brown hair was tied up over her head. She sat down a glass of wine. One of those glasses without a stem; Angel liked those the most.

"Oh, wow," she said, far too loudly for bein' normal. "Bart, you all came in through that door so fast it felt like you just appeared. Thanks fer coming by. Here, I'd like to talk to you."

Quickly, Angel led the group out into the backyard.

"You ok?" she asked. "I can put you upstairs if you need."

Tom waved enthusiastically, and Old had jumped back into the bag. Horse was hanging her head, and even the sprites were out of view.

"Oh, thanks, but I'm fine. Horse had too much a somethin' at the holiday party with our gaming friends, and now she can't port us back proper."

Angel's face scrunched, the way it always did when she was up for lecturing. But then she didn't say whatever she was going to.

"See ya, Bart." She rested a hand on Horse's flank and then walked back into the house.

Old had appeared in front of them. "It's time to get to bed, Bart. I think Horse has got it now, anyway."

Bart hoped so. They were sure getting tired.

Adjusting their hat, they walked through one more portal, expecting a cloud world or a big casino or bein' at the bottom of the ocean or something. What they saw was a bed. Bart walked to the window of the small room, and saw Horse outside, her head down into a trough. Tom was glowing on the ground as if trying to sleep, and the sprites hovered around. A small spot, like a star, blinked brightly on Horse's flank, changing between a deep blue and brighter white, about where Angel had patted her.

"It's a portal artifact," Old said, sitting over on the round table. "She made too many portals at once, so a little piece stuck on her."

Bart worried. "Is she alright?"

"Alright?" Old chuckled. "She said it's the best bling she's ever had. Loves it."

"Oh." Bart looked at the bed.

"I'm going to bed now, Bart. See you in the mornin'?"

"Yeah," Bart said. "Hey Old. That was a great party. We really have the best friends."

"We do," Old agreed. "Good night, Bart."

"Good night."

Coworkers

"Bart was just tryn'ta get some work . . ."

By the time Bart woke up, the new year was well upon them.

And they needed to earn some coin. "Nothing weird today," they muttered, running a washcloth over their face and neck. "No horsetowns, no robots, no parties. Just a solid job and solid day's work."

Lettin' Old stay back, Bart walked out to the back of the inn, where the rising sun cast a calming glow over the restless plains. They took a long breath in, and then out.

Horse was still asleep, it seemed. They didn't see the sprites, but they'd gotten a sense those sprites could take care of themselves. Real or not.

Only Tom was up, staring off at the sun, unusually wistful. They didn't argue when he trailed along, as Bart sauntered up the dusty main street.

Like mosta' these places, the Town Hall looked to be where folks lookin' for work had gathered.

"None of you have done framing?" the stout mayor was saying.

Bart hustled up closer. "I've done lotsa framing," they offered. "Buildings, interiors, trim. Even a picture or a few." Bart grinned, but no one laughed.

"Perfect!" the mayor said, letting a sigh that sounded a little like Horse. "Are you available to work today?" He—he wore the traditional he-get-up of a town like this and no pin—pointed down at lumpy bags. "Gold coins in there, *ample* gold coins, if we can get the job done today."

Bart stared at the bags. If those were really full a'gold, that was more pay than he'd be used to. "If it's possible, I'll do my best to make it happen."

"Great!" the mayor said, his face brightening. Bart had a sudden feeling one of those bags would be staying back here. Made sense; a good agent's time was valuable.

"It must be built today for the client, while his wife is away on work. It's a surprise. Now, here's the whole team." He pointed toward a group.

Team?

Now, look. Bart liked teams just fine. But Bart was takin' some time off from the grind, and just wanted a solid day of work with a solid feeling of non-drama. "Coworkers," they muttered. Then, to the mayor, "Alright, then, who's in charge?"

"Oh, you'll all work together. I don't want to cause any tension by putting someone in charge."

Bart and Tom exchanged glances. That was not — how it worked. They glanced again at that bag of gold. Horse was still hungover. Might be nice to take her out tonight.

They sighed. "Well, what are we building? Surprise? That sounds fun."

"It's a She-Shed!" The mayor beamed, kinda forced.

Bart knew their mouth had turned into as much of a

straight line as Old's little marker face could'a made. They almost stepped back, but Tom shook his head.

Muck on my boots. "Uh, I heard about those. Hangouts. Sounds fun. But, er, did this wife *request* a she-shed or is this his idea?"

"We do what we get paid to do, right?"

That was … true enough. With a grimace. Well, look, it was a rush project. There was a bag of gold and a group waiting. At least they could make a nice shed. Everyone deserved a space.

Bart moseyed up to the group as they walked off, away from town.

"I'm Bart," they said. "They/them." Bart tapped their pronoun pin. "You?"

The others all muttered their names, all with variations of, "Oh, I'm just he."

Now if you knew anything about just-he-sorts, you knew they were anything but just. Bart didn't go there. "So, we have no women working on the she-shed?"

"Makes sense, doesn't it? Building takes heft!"

No. It made no sense.

"Welcome to being the bad guy," one said.

Oh no. Bart knew where this was going. But yet, one of the others still asked.

"What do you mean?"

Bart winced.

"It's like you can't even get work anymore if you're a man, you know? You know what I mean, Bart?"

Extra peppers. Why do they always get brought into it?

"Actually, I'd say it doesn't seem to be a problem, looking at this group."

"You're not a man, right?"

Prince save me. "Correct. But you hired me because you were missing a skill. Now, look, maybe this she-shed thing has got us all feelin' funny. Let's just get to work, get it built, and go back and get our coins. Agree?"

The men all nodded. Good.

Achoo.

One man had just sneezed right into Bart's wind. Bart slowed down, getting out of range, and rubbing on some hand sanitizer.

The guy gave them a glare, like they were being unfriendly. Well this day could be over soon.

Turned out, though, once they got to the couple's backyard and the sun rose high and it was a beautiful, breezy day, Bart was able to lean into the spirit of it. They'd just pulled over several bundles of lumber, and picked the right sizes and strength for the sort of structure they'd need. The others were talking design.

"We'll put it in the garden, I think. So we'll need to clear all this out."

Bart scanned the area. Whoever this wife was, she sure seemed to love her gardens.

"We don't need to destroy her garden. I'd say we build it off to the side. Let there be gardens around it. Maybe some trellises."

"I suppose that makes sense," one mused. "Why don't we integrate the garden with the shed. Seems she'd like that."

Bart tried to ignore that, but another man had moved over.

"You look handsome today." He gave a grin.

"Just here to do a job," Bart replied. Seemed nice enough, but anyone who couldn't wait more than 600 words to make a move was not drama Bart needed.

"Well, I'm saying if you don't have a place to go when we're done—"

Bart cut this off. "And I'm sayin' we've got to build a whole shed in one day, so we'd best focus on that."

"So I saw this idea for a rustic hot cocoa bar," another had started. "We take some of that weathered crate wood, sand it down and paint it, like this is a tiny cocoa shop. We can paint 'Cocoa Shop, Five Cents', but with the little cent sign."

"Sure, but we don't know her preferences," Bart worked in. "Why not just make a fabulous bar area, then she can serve whatever she likes." Bart tried to picture this woman makin' martinis under the cocoa sign—just having to look at that thing all day even when she was sweating from her garden. "Probably don't want to get too specific if we don't know the folk."

The flirty one came to their defense, and the other relented. Few minutes later, they had a real sleek bar designed up, and Bart was going to frame some nice, versatile cabinets, to install once the walls were up.

"Who's laying stone?" they asked. "I reckon the patio would draw out around this way." They traced it out, pointing with a long stick.

"He didn't say it needed a patio."

Bart sighed. "On a nice day like today, if the boss came by with a six-pack *of beer*—" They wanted that clarified for the flirty fella. "—would we all go sit in the shed together?"

The men exchanged glances. "There were some tiles in the supplies," one said. "They'll work fine." He hefted the wheelbarrow and took off that way.

"Right, then," another said. "So I think we're ready to get the bones up."

Bart winced.

"Bart, right? When you frame it out, let's do a fake wall. The owner has some old bike parts that might come in handy, and he asked about combining—"

"No." Bart literally stomped a foot. "No. If the *wife* has old bike parts, then I will gladly frame out a cabinet or a side workshop, or whatever. But we are not storing his things in her shed when the shed is a gift for her. I just have to put my foot down." Realizing they already had, they stood in place awkwardly. "Here's what I suggest—"

One of the men had interrupted. Patiently, Bart waited until he'd stopped, then tried again.

"Here's what I suggest—"

Another took over, going on about honoring the customer and we'll just make it a little larger. Bart had seen this show before.

Bellowing up more solidly than they liked to, Bart started in, continuing to talk until the others realized they were not going to stop this time.

They restarted. "Here's what I suggest. The customer

asked for storage. I'm a fast framer. I'll make a nice cabinet, out of view of this, over by the house. Bike parts will be stored, and, shed folk gets her own damn shed."

Oops. Getting talked over sometimes made Bart get salty.

Tom glowed brightly. Bart almost high-fived him, but one, high-fiving a ghost can feel sort of gross, and two, no one else could see him so it'd look right dramatic.

Bart was surprised to hear, barely hear, a neigh in the distance. Oh, Horse must have found them. They bet those sprites were here too.

"The customer was very specific," one offered. "This was for her, not for both of them. It's a gift."

"Very specific," another agreed.

"It's not a they-house," the stone guy quipped, back now with the patio stones.

Now that caught Bart's interest. But this wasn't the point. "Listen. If he didn't want it to be for him, he shouldn't'a brought his bike parts into it. I'm a fast framer. Let me get to work, and I promise everyone will be happy. Iffen you let me work."

Bart went over to check out the pile of bike parts. Some of them were pretty nice; Bart could see hanging on to these. You never know when you'll get time for a project.

Horse had walked over and nudged Bart's arm. Bart almost said *Hey* but remembered sometimes Horse was sensitive about that. They thought it was a bit much, but it never hurt Bart to think of others when choosing their words.

"Howdy," Bart said. Horse was sniffing around a pile of metal scrap, off to the side.

"Why is there a horse here?" One of the men had joined them.

"She's my friend." Bart almost did an introduction, but they hadn't quite caught all their names. "This pile, does this go in the cabinet too?" Maybe Bart could craft out some drawers.

"No, no. That's all scrap from the old shed. I was asked to take it down to the dumpster hole."

Those dumpsters always sounded less acceptable when the dumping part was noted, but Bart had enough to worry about lately.

Horse was pointing right at a shiny little garden bell, with old, worn engraving. Well, if it was going in the trash. They picked it up and winked at Horse, who neighed softly as Bart slipped it on her. The bell rested just between Horse's sparkly lanyard with the Wizard Dice clipped on and their Tournament Medal.

Soon, Bart was able to get to work. The parts cabinet came together real nice, and the group had barely got the floor in place by the time Bart came back to start walls. So it all worked out.

The structure being basic enough, Bart had talked them into a few more windows and a steeper roof—nothing Bart couldn't do in their sleep. Not really. That just meant Bart was good at framing. Sort of a proud thing, you know.

The walls were going up great, and Horse helped lift a few into place.

"I need to run and get some paint," one of the coworkers was saying. "White paint I suppose. Need that for shabby chic. It'll match the gauzy curtains."

For what?

"Now, look," Bart tipped their hat. "I've meddled in this enough for today, but if I could just offer a suggestion."

The others waited. Well, that was nice.

"White curtains and paint will get dirty right fast. Would you want that?"

"No," they said in mostly unison. "But we're not shes."

Bart cringed. "I know, me neither. But I don't think dirty curtains are a gendered thing." Bart didn't think much of this was a gendered thing, but folk sure got into all that.

To Bart's surprise, they decided on a soft blue, to complement the shades of the garden. And didn't argue when Bart asked for a can of lavender. For the little steeple they'd added.

Well, it was a lot of framing, and people had to start painting while Bart was still finishing the roof, and then someone brought in shingles and started tacking those up, and by the time twilight peeked over the pond, Bart felt like one of those flashy improvement shows where the work is so shoddy the residents have to use their show fees to get it all replaced.

'Cept none of this was shoddy. Not a bit. This was one fine . . . shed. Bart would just call it that.

"Hooooowdy!" A man with a giant belt buckle that certainly must be the husband strode back toward the work area. A younger folk trailed behind him, pulling a cart with the bags of money. Bart tipped their hat, though not too dramatically, since they were still on the roof. Just about done, though.

And as the man had just about finished inspecting the place, Bart climbed down and walked over. They hoped he liked it.

"Why is there a horse in my front yard? And where are my bike parts?"

Bart grimaced. Best to focus this. "They're in a cabinet, over there. Here, let me show you." Nervously, Bart walked him over.

"This is fantastic!"

"Yeah," Bart hastened to agree. "We thought so. And if you want, you have room on this side for a workshop. You know, for when you get to that big project."

The man slapped Bart across the back, almost knocking them over. "You're sure right about that! You're the framer?"

"I am." Bart took a cloth from their pocket and wiped their forehead.

"The interior team will take it from here. They're coming in for the night. Everything should be good to go. A right and proper she-shed!"

"Uh, yeah," Bart said. "Sure."

And soon after, Bart, tired and glad the coworkers weren't much for goodbyes, wandered back out to the road where, Horse, now talking to Tom, was waiting. Bart tipped their hat to Twinkle and Sparkle, who sprayed some imaginary glitter in response. Old was suddenly at Bart's side, looking livelier than Bart felt. Horse, on the other hand, still didn't look her best. Bart knew a fix for that.

"Now that we've got the posse," Bart said, sorta to everyone, "you, uh, want to go out for margaritas?"

Horse lifted her head enthusiastically, the little bell jingling.

"Sure thing," Tom said. The sprites danced. Only Old looked slightly nervous.

"With a side of whiskey," Bart reassured. Old's little marker mouth spread into an upturned arc.

"You got it," it said.

As Bart turned to leave, they caught a glance of the new shed as the evening light glowed off of the fresh paints. Maybe she-sheds weren't so bad. Maybe someday when this was all over, Bart would get that they-house.

Something in the sunset caught in their eyes, and with a sigh, they walked off, posse close by.

Haunted Town

"A ghostly experience . . . "

Everyone was feeling great, Bart had made a few coins, and the sun was rising over—

Bart looked out of the window. The sun was not rising. The whole town seemed to have been shrouded in a swirling pearlescent fog.

"Damn." They rubbed the side of their head.

Now, a hero might rush out and figure out what was going on, but Bart's heroism sometimes required a touch of caffeine and hygiene. This inn had a terrific shower, and an in-room coffee grinder and kettle. If today was Bart's last day of livin' then they were sure to start with a cup of that coffee.

Turning the crank on the little grinder, Bart worked out some nice dark grounds. They shook them into the filter cup, poured in water from the pitcher, and set the thing on the fire, once they got that goin' too.

By the time they finished up down the hall in that shower and took a sip of coffee, they'd almost forgotten that the world had gone to fog outside.

Whelp. It still had.

"Know anything about that?" they asked Old.

"I had nothing to do with that," Old whispered. "I don't know." Seeming frightened, it hopped into Bart's satchel.

Bart put their hat back on, switched into the clothes the innkeep had been kind enough to launder, grabbed their bag, and headed out to see what in speculative fiction was goin' on out there.

It was odd walking. But the ground seemed to be in place, and Bart could breathe just fine. Slowly, making sure not to bump anything, they made their way to the stable. Horse was there, lookin' chipper enough, playing some sort of card game with the sprites. "Horse. Twinkle. Sparkle." Bart tipped their hat at each. "So, uh, interesting morning?"

Horse snorted and flipped a card over with her hoof. Even her gold hoof covers looked duller in the thickness of the air.

"Horses aren't afraid of ghosts," Twinkle offered.

Bart stepped back a bit.

"That's what these are," she continued. "Someone opened a ghost portal and now the town's full of them."

"Alright." Bart adjusted their hat. "Do they, er, go home? After a bit?"

"I don't know. We're sprites so it's not real to us. And Horse doesn't care."

Bart cared. What, were they . . . breathin' in ghost bodies right now? Holy Cher.

Speaking of ghosts, though. "Where's Tom?"

"Haven't seen him," Sprinkle said. "Not since it started."

Bart opened their bag and saw Old hiding in the bottom. "Old, you ok?"

"Yeah, but I'd rather stay in here for now."

"Sure, Old. Do you know where Tom went?"

Old didn't. And it just kept insisting it wasn't part of this. The whiskey bottle had been acting funny lately, Bart realized. Something to look into when they weren't surrounded by ghosts. Either way, Bart realized they were on their own for this one.

They walked out to the Main Street, thinking there might be some signs, anyway, in a place with a ghost portal. But no one was out. Folk seemed right spooked by it.

Bart was starting to feel a touch spooked themself. "Tom," they called out. "Tom, you around?"

It was a surprising relief when the bloopy little ghost shape popped into view. Not swirly and surreal like the rest of whatever was going on, but cute and . . . formed. Or whatever.

"Tom, I'm glad to see you."

Tom glowed brightly.

"Do you know what's going on?"

"I do, actually. Look, ghost portals are serious for us. I don't want to leave. I want to be here. And sometimes if a portal's open too long, a ghost might come in or stay . . . out." Now he looked worried. A ghost shape without features can't really turn around so much, but Bart got the impression that's what he was conveying, that he was scanning around. And Bart realized another thing. They weren't used to seeing Tom scared.

"Is it safe. To go there?"

"I think if you're with me," Tom muttered.

Aww, well Bart wasn't used to hearing things like that from Tom. It warmed them a touch.

Together, they walked—well Bart walked and Tom floated—down the street and back across a side street to a little circle of nice, simple homes. "That one," Tom whispered.

Bart knocked at the door. No one answered.

Well, Bart didn't know what to do. They weren't about to barge into someone's home, but yet there sure was nothing tolerable about breathin' in a swirl of ghosts, and with their friends scared—

Tom floated in through the door. A few seconds later, a young sort came running through the front door. Well, in this case, the door was opened, Bart should clarify.

"I don't even know this one! And who are you?"

"I'm Bart. They/them." They tapped their brassy pin.

"Oh. Jared. He/him." He huffed in place. "I'm sorry, this is all my fault. My . . . grandma is in there."

"Alright." Bart could see where this was going. "And she's uh—" They waved a hand around.

"Yeah. Dead. Or at least I thought she was. Until I started my own gaming brand. 'Jared Lightning'."

"Is that your name? So that's a family issue now?"

"No. It's not my name. It's cooler than my name." Jared suddenly swung the door open and howled inside. "I'm allowed to play games. I'm allowed to be alive now that you're dead, and I can call myself whatever I want."

Bart was seeing this was more serious than they thought. "Here, want to go talk to her? I'll stay with you. Sometimes, you just need a friend."

"Yeah. Ok." Jared stomped into the house and plopped down on a well-used couch with a few blankets strewn over it. Tom was looking nervously toward a quite solid appari-tion of a woman. She didn't look like a grandma, per se. Bart wasn't judging anyone's dress, but she was quite young, is all they meant.

"Bart, this is my grandma, Grandma. She shows up my age."

She put her hands on her hips. "Well you think I'm going to float in with my dad's arthritis if I don't have to?"

"Hello, there, uh, Ms. Grandma. I'm Bart." They tipped their hat. "Seein' as you're dead, is there a reason why you can't just let Jared start a game company?"

"It's embarrassing! After all the years I worked long shifts and wrecked my joints, and now what he's going to play games all day? Now, you have nothing to do with this. Go on!"

Yeah, Bart had their own issues in the family, but haunting a whole town over perceptions of meritocracy was a thing where a fella might need some support. Everyone needed a posse for that sort of thing. They thought of their own grandma, quiet and with a euphemism for *everything*. They did miss her.

"What? Who brought me down here?"

"Marma!" Bart staggered back. "Well, Jared here opened a ghost portal, and his grandma's givin' him shit, and I thought about how much I missed you, and—"

Marma glanced between Grandma, Tom, Jared, and Bart. Her eyes rested on their chest. "They/them!"

Oh, no. Bart didn't need to—

"Oh, that's fantastic! Being fancy has run in the family a while, but people had occupations to keep."

Bart winced, hoping Marma wasn't going to ask about theirs. She didn't.

"But I moved along. And don't see any reason why I need to be here. My fine grandchild is beautiful and doesn't need to deal with my warts on top of their own."

"Marma," Bart muttered.

"Well, no one asked you here!" Grandma said, seeming to catch her bearings. "At least your grandchild is a sheriff; mine is off besmirching the family legacy with Satanic propaganda!"

I'm not a—

"Gaming is storytelling," Jared shouted, jumping to his feet. "It is the oldest and best thing in the world."

"Except for the horizontal exercise!" Marma interjected. Bart pretended they didn't hear.

"You know—you know what the *worst* part of this is?" Jared was getting a fire in his eyes. "Is that you're dead. It was bad enough to get judged all the time when you were here, but you're not even here, and you're still trying to control me. Grandma, I love you, but—"

Grandma grew to about twice the size. Even Marma floated back.

"You love me?"

Jared glanced to Bart, and Bart could only gesture him on.

"Yeah. Of course I do. I love you and I miss you. And that's why it hurts extra that I'm finally doing what speaks to my soul, and—"

Jared slumped back onto the couch. Like he couldn't continue.

Bart and Marma met eyes. She nodded them on.

"Grandma?" they offered tentatively. "When a folk is doing something that stirs their very soul, it's like leaving that soul exposed out on the parlor table like a fresh crochet for everyone to inspect. And it's times like those that a folk best needs a posse. I don't know, I just don't know, who Jared has right now. And . . . I don't know if he has you."

The room fell silent. Outside, Bart could hear the howling of ghosts. Tom was growing fainter. Bart didn't know what to do.

"Lightning." Grandma said it, then stopped.

Jared turned away.

"Is a damn cool name I wish I'd have had. Margery. Margery . . ."

Bart tried to smile encouragingly.

"Punchbowl won't empty itself," Marma whispered.

Grandma shrunk down to normal size, and for a moment she looked to be the age of maybe . . . of maybe when Jared was born.

"Margery Lightning. A fine woman that would have been."

Again, they waited in silence.

"I learned a lot from you, Grandma," Jared started. "Who you were—is part of me now. When I wake up in the morning, when I make my coffee strong, when I sing your song—when no one's watching—I feel you. Not within me, but as part of me. Part of me, part of my magic, part of my spark. Grandma, I would invite you on this journey with me, but the truth is, you're already there. Your acceptance? There are some magics I simply can't conjure." He looked up, but now there was a light in his eyes. "I am a simple bard. And in that, I am content."

Now that was a gamer monologue if Bart had ever heard one. And they didn't need to see the roll. Sure, they might have watched Margery for her reaction, but instead they turned to Marma. She wouldn't be here much longer, they suspected, and they'd missed her. And showing her their pin. That meant a lot. Bart sighed, a little of the weight escaping.

As Bart rested into Marma's eyes, the most peace Bart had had in a long while settled into their own. Into their heart. Down into their fingers and toes.

Marma knew.

And Jared and Margery had some kind of farewell, or settled something, and all Bart could do was watch Marma one last time.

No. Not a last time. Marma was still in Bart, too.

"Bart," Marma whispered, as if they were alone in a room where no one else could hear. "I'm proud of you. I know it's hard. You'll be ok. I promise."

Bart wasn't sure how she could promise that.

Marma smiled. "Oh, I can. You know how I know? You're ok now."

Now, all hell, Bart was not going to stand here and cry. They closed their eyes, and soon the air was clear and Tom was the only ghost in the room, and even he looked . . . different. Less of a ghost. More of a companion. Softer.

And Bart was standing in the middle of some fella's living room. With a look at the folk, glowing with a fuller buff than reality could offer, Bart realized there was no goodbye here. Bart tipped their hat and let themself back outside.

Old had appeared in front of them, but not so animated as usual. With a gentle nod, Bart walked back to find Horse and the sprites.

If there was a moment to be shared, it wasn't here.

Horse was guffawing, the way a horse might do it, and the sprites were giggling up a storm.

"I took care of the ghost thing."

Sparkle glanced up. "Whatever. We had the *best* time. Humans weren't bothering us, and we could play glitter games . . . just sort of sorry it's over."

See, that was one thing about sprites of ambiguous realness. They didn't always see reality. Fact was, it was never over. Just maybe sometimes it was easier.

Bart wasn't going to take away anyone's happy without cause. "Well, good," they said, trying to put on a smile. "I'm sure glad you had a fine time. What did you do?"

"A fairy door!" Twinkle said, pointing down at Horse's hoof. They'd cut into one of Horse's gold hoof skirts, tying it back like a curtain. And behind that, well, Sweet Annie, there was some sort of . . . door. Glued onto her hoof. And tufts of moss? And a little picture frame.

"Oh, I see," Tom said, floating down. "It's a fairy door."

Tom looked rather happy. Old was staring off toward the town. Horse nuzzled Bart's arm, seeming content. And so Bart did the thing they could think to do.

"That's a fine fairy door, Horse. I'm right proud of you."

Oh. Bart had almost forgotten the best part. They stared right at Horse. Right at Tom. "I'm glad you're you."

Just Bart: Episode 19

Staying In

"An unexpected turn . . ."

The coins were low again, but with that ghost issue resolved and some word of mouth from an appreciative Jared, Bart had lined up solid work in this town that would last them a good while, maybe even get them out of the real ghost town they'd suffered these last years. Things were finally looking up.

A note slid under Bart's doorway, across the wood planks of their cozy room.

Bart, it began. *We've received word that a sickness is spreading across our town. All folk must stay in their rooms until we send additional word. If you must leave for an emergency, kindly stay a horse's length away from any other human. Otherwise, please stay where you are.*

This was the kinda thing that took a minute to sink in.

After washing their hands at the washstand, Bart walked over to the window, up on the third floor. They could see Horse outside, along with Tom, Sparkle, and Twinkle. They all looked well, but didn't seem to notice Bart, up at the window. Bart felt a little separated from them already, but wasn't the sort to holler.

Old was here, in the room. Bart tried to let it sleep, for now.

For a little bit, Bart just sat on the low bed. Not bein'

at home, Bart didn't have their books. There was a pad o' paper on the nightstand and a small charcoal pencil. They supposed they could draw a picture.

They weren't ready yet to draw a picture. Maybe that was an odd thing to say, but it's easy to tell someone to relax, and sometimes much harder to do it. Instead, they tapped the pencil against the pad, scratching out a quick note:

Hello, innkeepers in this here town,

I will surely comply and do what I can to help keep folk safe. But could I ask—is there any way I could help? I don't know much about medicine, but I'm good at framing wood. And software design.

With a wince, they added, *and V&V.*

Thanks. Bart. (they/them)

Just as they slid the note under the door, a zapping noise sounded, nearly scaring them into a backflip.

Bart couldn't really do a backflip; they just felt like it the way they got startled, sometimes.

The purple shape was a bit like a mage portal, but small. And kinda' wavy. *Ah.* Bart suddenly realized what this was. And they were pretty sure who made it. "Howdy?" they said into the portal.

Sure enough, MageBoss' face appeared, wavy like a you're my last hope sort of deal. While the last time they'd seen per, per'd been dressed in fancy wizard robes, this time per was only wearing matching pants and a shirt. And they were ... fuzzy. With a pattern of little coffee mugs.

"Bart! I wanted to see how you were doing."

That was a nice thing to hear.

"I'm alright. Horse and Tom are down there." Bart pointed out to the back prairie. They would have mentioned the sprites, but MageBoss knew all about them and it was still a touchy subject.

"Oh, I was already down there."

"Like, one of these view-portals?"

"Nah, I actually teleported over. Horses and ghosts can't catch people stuff. Didn't want to worry the townfolk, though, so I just left them some playthings and then ported back to the tower."

Playthings? What playthings would both Horse and Tom enjoy? Tom couldn't even hold objects.

They went to peer out of the window. Apparently ghosts *could* hold objects? The damn rules were so inconsistent Bart was starting to think they were never real in the first place. Maybe none of this was real.

Then, whatever large silvery can Tom had in his ... grasp sprayed out a stream of brassy glitter. Right onto Horse's side. One, two, then three big glittery stripes across her soft brown flank.

Bart knew Horse could handle herself, but what the hay was going on out there?

A *swoosh* sounded under the door. Another note.

Mx. Bart,

We appreciate your offer kindly, but with your specialties and these timelines, it would be best to stay in. You should have what you need in your room, and the rooms nearby are empty, so you'll have the washroom to yourself. You can cook on your stove, and we'll offer a kitchen drop-off service later.

Thanks for your understanding. Stay safe.

Bart stared at the note. Things sure could change right fast. They threw the note into the fireplace and had just washed their hands again when MageBoss reappeared in the view-portal.

"Did you give Horse glitter paint? Is that safe?"

"You worry so much, Bart."

"How can I not be worried right now?"

"Fair point." Per gazed off at something or somewhere out of Bart's view. "You have a tablet at least? Magic mirror?"

"Huh? No. It's just me and Old." Bart glanced again at the whiskey bottle, right now just looking like an old bottle with a torn label. He pictured its little marker-drawn face, and—

"Hey. You up for playing a game?"

Bart wasn't so sure. "I don't know. That's nice to offer, but it can be hard to relax into a game, not with this kind of feeling. Hey, how's Sal?"

MageBoss paused. "She's not feeling well. But I keep checking back with her. She's sleeping now. Maybe … maybe *I* could use a game. We could walk into it?"

If per needed a game, that sure gave Bart a reason to give it a try. "Alright. What game? Nothing too complicated," they added. "I just don't have the brain for it."

Look, situation or not, MageBoss had a penchant for some overly complicated games.

Bart sat back on the bed and the portal spun to adjust. Bart glanced at Old.

"Did you ever go camping?" per asked.

Bart had more stories on that than there was time to get into. "Yes."

"Ever play a story game? You know, one wizard starts, then the next one goes."

They hadn't specifically camped with wizards, but they also supposed that wasn't the point. "I know how to play that. But, would you start?"

MageBoss' mouth turned up with a slight grin. That was nice to see. Until now, Bart hadn't really noticed how down MageBoss had been looking. Maybe that was a side effect of being in this little room, 'n it was harder to see everyone else. But they were still there. In some ways, they felt closer.

Clearing per throat, per began. "A wizard stands at the edge of a harried town, lightning sparking from the sparkling ruby at the crest of eir burlwood staff, as the screeching goblins turned and raced away from the helpless village."

Bart was just a simple folk, and did not know a lot about wizards. Not even getting into that goblins they'd met had been quite a different sort. It did feel a little extreme, to jump right in with attackin' a town when they were trying to relax. *Well.* They scratched the side of their head—their hat was over on the stand—and tried to figure how to add to such a grand scene. *That's it. Make it grander.*

"Eir name was Firefoot," Bart said, solemnly.

MageBoss drew per mouth into a thin line and sat straighter. "Firefoot, the almighty! With fierce skill and power, e wards off the vile creatures, as the people of the village cheer eir name!"

"Firefoot!" Bart added. You know, the cheering of eir

name. MageBoss didn't seem to take this as the next line, though, so Bart scrambled to come up with something. Ok. Wizards. That was fantasy. Wizards and . . . dragons. Right. Dragons always help with fantasy. Bart beamed a bit, proud o' this part.

"A flapping sounds across the yonder hills." They pointed up for effect. "A fine, slate gray dragon, colored like the far reach of a rocky trail, soars across toward Firefoot." Bart lowered their hand.

MageBoss raised pers. "Firefoot casts minor illusion," per boomed, "augmenting emself into a huge vision reaching up into the crackling sky and toward the approaching beast. 'You shall not harm the people of this innocent village!' e declares."

"'I would harm no one,' the dragon said, with a voice like a fine evenin' fiddle, as the dragon landed softly on a patch of moss. Firefoot moseyed forward. 'I am the wizard Firefoot, e/em. Fine dragon, to what do I owe this pleasure?'" Bart was startin' to get the hang of this.

MageBoss' eyes narrowed. "A plume of orange fire burst from the creature's toothy maw, and Firefoot cast a glittering shield of ice, blocking its barrage."

"'Excuse me,' the dragon crowed. 'Seltzer water always gives me the burps, and the magic stream of the elves where I have just availed of a sip flows with magic bubbles. Now, fine Firefoot. You may call me Dragon. Any pronouns will do. What is it that you are doing here, casting lightning into our gentle skies?'"

There was a long pause. Through the waving portal,

MageBoss looked to be rubbing per temples. "Bart. I'm trying to create a heroic story here. I'm not sure we've quite synched."

Now, see, Game Masters were the best of us, and they meant that truly, but sometimes they forgot that folk watered their own gardens.

"I think we're doing great," they said. "But can't the dragon be friendly?"

The wizard sat back, pixelating momentarily in the view-portal. "You know, fine, it's friendly." Per changed per tone of voice. "'Ah! You must be the famed village dragon! If you turn to the windbreak of this small village, you will see a wall of goblins, just nearly turned away, running back toward the haytopped hamlet.' The dragon turned and recoiled at the foul sight. 'I will help you save them,' she cried."

Bart rubbed their hands together. Now, this was teamwork. "'Dearest goblins, you are scaring the villagers. Is there something you seek? A way that we can help?'"

Getting into it now, Bart hardly noticed when Old joined them, its little face adding little eyebrows, that rose in anticipation.

MageBoss' voice for the goblins made Bart jump in place, as per called out: "'There is nothing! We have finally found the village that harbored the Dark Light of Obsidian, and it will now be ours!'"

"'Well, it's darn rude!' the dragon said. 'Now, why don't we sit down together, talk about this magic piece of glass, and maybe work something out!'" Bart liked diplomatic solutions.

But MageBoss only sighed. After closing per eyes tight for a moment, per opened them. "'What's that?' Firefoot called out. A glowing purple light emitted from the edge of the haunted forest. Seeing it, nearby townpeople shrieked, and ran back into their dwellings. 'We'll save you!' Firefoot bellowed as eir dragon went to negotiate like Bart with the goblins."

Now, per didn't need to fly off their dragon. But a mystery portal did sound like a good adventure they could both make work. They met MageBoss' eyes and was glad when per broke into a warm grin.

"We should definitely go check that out," Bart agreed. "I mean, Firefoot is brave and rushes to check out the magic portal. E steps in, and lands in—"

Bart never knew what these things were supposed to be. A maze, or a multi-dimensional castle maybe, or—

"A treasure room." MageBoss' voice took on a smoky mystery. "But not just any room. A puzzle room, glowing in radiant glowing light, with dire consequences should the brave and clever wizard fail."

Puzzles. "Alex Trebek," Bart blurted out. "Alex Trebek is there, guarding the magical treasure."

"Alex Trebek?"

"You know, the fella on that show—*Peril* or something?—where all the old folk think he's so appropriate 'account of sounding so polite, but if you ever wanted a masterclass on epic sarcasm—"

"No, I know who he is. Though I never saw what was

perilous about answering unobtrusive questions you can only profit from. He's in our story?"

"I do believe that's fair use. And you don't answer questions, you know, you actually ask them."

MageBoss squinted, then grinned again. "Ok. We'll come up with some questions, er, answers, and if we can get through the question labyrinth we'll find the treasure and deliver it to the villagers."

"And that will solve what the goblins are looking for."

"Sure, Bart. This sounds fun. And when Sal's awake, I'll port her in and we can all talk about it."

Bart rested a hand over Old, before taking a sip of whiskey from a glass that was etched with the logo of the inn: a flickering hearth. "Old, you wanna go first?"

"I sure will," Old said, spinning in place.

Bart watched it a moment, then looked up at MageBoss. "You know, I almost forgot about . . . all this for a moment." The wizard would know what they meant.

"That's what stories do, friend. Sometimes they help us imagine, but sometimes they help us forget. Just a little. Now, we don't want to keep the Guardian Wizard Alex Trebek waiting, do we?"

With another sip of whiskey, Bart realized they were smiling. Like, for real smiling. The way Angel always did. They hoped she was well now. Maybe MageBoss could check on her, you know, without needin' to say Bart was behind it. They looked back into the portal, where MageBoss was tossing a wizard-fired dice in per hand.

"Let's do Potpourri, but actually make it about potpourri."

"You got it, friend."

Bart had always appreciated folk. But the next time Bart got out to be together, they had a feeling they might appreciate them even a little more.

Just Bart: Episode 20

Fantasy Land

"Things are a lot . . ."

It was hard lately.

Working job-to-job had been a lot as it were, and then on top of that, when the sickness came, Bart lost all the jobs they'd finally lined up. Seemed selfish to think about coins when there was so much suffering around them, but how was a folk ever supposed to relax when they had to keep tapping at an imaginary button just to do basic things?

Horse and Tom were quiet too, as they walked together down an empty road. Old was asleep in the bag. Only the sprites seemed unaffected.

"I told you, it's because we're not real. Can't be affected by things if you aren't real," one said.

Bart didn't think that was right. "You know, this whole thing might be getting weirder than I intended it," they muttered.

"Weird is a euphemism, Bart."

"What?" You know, never mind. Bart had no camp cups to be arguing with sprites. "Well, fine, what are you fixin' we do?"

"Let's find a fantasy land."

"Are we talking about a story? Or an actual place?"

Horse sniffed the air, then started trotting, away from

the road and toward a distant arc of wood. A bridge, Bart supposed, but over what?

Turned out, the bridge was over a winding river that somehow existed in the dry plains, and on the other side were grassy hills and tall, waving shrubs.

A young child sat on a rock, presenting as a boy. He cried into his hands.

Bart rushed forward, but kept a distance. "Hello, I'm Bart. They/them. And this is Horse." Bart would have introduced the rest, but it was never clear who saw whom. "Can I help you with anything?"

The little boy sniffed. "I'm Wen. And something's wrong with our King."

Look, Bart was not a monarchy sort, but they also weren't into judging someone else's culture on an outside glimpse, so they kept that part to themself. "Howdy, Wen, would you tell me what's wrong with your King? Only if you're comfortable doing so, a' course."

"We used to get a daily allotment into each village: important supplies, coppers for each house. But now that's stopped. The coppers were always enough that we didn't have to be scared. We could get what we needed. But my mom hasn't been well, and finding work has been harder. I left home to try and find work, but everyone says I'm too little. And no one can understand what changed the King's mind; he's always done his best, Mom says."

Bart tried to imagine what that would be like: to always have enough coin to get by, even when times were tough.

To not have to worry about the next sunrise. They really couldn't. Not to say they couldn't, but they couldn't.

"You're saying the King supported this before, but now something has changed?"

"Yes." Wen took a quivering breath.

Horse stamped next to them. Bart agreed. Sounds like all they could do was go and investigate. Maybe helping someone else would distract Bart away from all they couldn't do right now.

Together, Wen led them down a winding path, and then a road, until a modest stone building came into view.

"Here is the castle."

Bart wasn't sure about a castle, it seemed more like an office building they'd worked in once in the Historical District, but they also supposed Fantasy Lands being surprising was part of the fun.

Leaving Wen nervously back, Bart and their posse approached the gate.

The guards tapped large spears onto the ground. "Have you an appointment?" one asked.

"We do not. I am a traveler from another land, and I wish to speak to your King about matters of import." Luckily, they'd learned some of this sort of talk from MageBoss. Bart pushed back a pang of sadness.

The guards shared an expression, and it rang confused. Yet they parted the gates. Slightly.

"The Horse must stay here."

Bart knew enough Horse talk to know when it was

Not Suitable For Castle, but either way, she nodded him forward, Tom hanging back with her.

Bart took a deep breath and walked toward the entrance. They probably should have taken a shower, but well, even Kings knew the road was tough. At least, it sounded like this one used to.

The castle, er, receptionist directed Bart to a row of plastic chairs. The waiting room was empty, which seemed strange for a King. In the stories Bart had read, there were always folk trying to be heard.

As they walked into the throne room, Bart stood a good ways away from the dais. The King was there, along with two counselors on each side, spaced apart.

The King wore a blue velvet outfit with a black-fringed cap. "As you were," he said.

Bart had no idea what that meant. "Yes, hello—how should I address you? I'm sorry; I'm not from here."

The King nodded curtly but without emotion. "King Daniel."

"Yes, howdy, King Daniel. I'm Bart, they/them, a traveler." They tipped their hat. "I learned some distressing news upon your land and was wondering if you were aware."

He sat forward. "No, do tell."

"Yes, well, the daily allotment to the villages has stopped. People who are struggling with health, or making art, or crossing an interruption in work suddenly have to worry about their basic needs."

"Many jobs are available," he said, drily. "If anyone needs

work, they can come here, to the Magrescity. Employment is always available."

Bart paused. That didn't sound right. You can't assign art. You can't assign health. "But, I—" Bart thought some more. If everyone had the opportunity to work, then all would be well.

"And charity. Charity cares for the weak," the King said.

That was true. There were always people eager to take care of others' needs. Bart smiled, apologized for the intrusion, and walked back through the doors and back out onto the road. Maybe Bart needed to find some charity. Surely, out there, there were—

They scratched their head. *Find charity?* What sort of burden was that to put on a person in need? And who's calling a fightin' folk weak? Their eyes blinked. Especially because two sprites were hovering right in front of them. Glitter burst out into their view like a burst garden hose, flapping around.

"That was some fucking dark magic," Sparkle burst out.

Twinkle looked too upset to talk.

Bart scratched their head. "Were you in there?"

"Yes, we were in there. One of those advisors is using a controlling rod on the King. It was used on you too!" Sparkle squinted, as if daring Bart to make them remind them it wouldn't work on things that weren't real.

"But why would anyone do that?" Bart wanted folk to have nice lives; who would prevent that?

Sparkle sighed. "When someone wants to stop someone

from havin' something nice, it's usually because they want to have more."

Bart stared ahead. "Alright. So this is our quest, right? Defeat the Rod of Control and bring reason back into the kingdom?"

Suddenly, Horse and Tom were back beside them. Old had popped out as well.

"Hey, Old," Bart said.

Its little marker face just looked worried. "I can't help with this one," it said, voice weaker than normal. "I'm here for you, but this is bigger than me."

"It's bigger than me, too, fellas, I just—"

They looked up at the silent sprite, her wings slowly flapping in what looked like a sad rhythm. "Twinkle? If you're willing to share, how would you work this?"

"You go back in there. If you can. And you let people know what's going on."

"But won't I just get mind-controlled again?"

Twinkle sighed. It was Tom who answered.

"That's the thing with mind-control. Once you see the dark magic, it no longer works on you. Usually, anyway." Tom's usual brightness had faded.

Bart glanced desperately between the posse. Something wasn't right. "I thought we found a fantasy land to get away from our worries. This story is sort'a . . . sad."

"Sometimes when you're sad," Old murmured, "there's no easy happy. But that doesn't mean you won't find it again."

Bart didn't like the way that all made them feel. But

they were not going to be controlled by no dangnabbed *rod* and maybe that was what they could do for now.

With Horse whinnying heroically behind them, Bart marched back up toward the castle gate. As they neared, Wen hurried to their side.

They didn't want to burden a child with such things. But here he was, tears on his face. The burden wasn't the dark magic. The burden was its effects.

"I think someone is controlling the King. And I think I know what to do. I'll be back soon, ok?"

Wen nodded, and Bart marched forward.

"I request to speak to King Daniel," they said, tipping their hat at each guard.

"The King is done with petitions today."

Bart grimaced. "He's wonderful, isn't he?"

The guards nodded. "Yes, he gets things done."

"Yes, so many things," Bart agreed. And they continued to banter as Bart wiggled open the gate and slipped through, breaking into a run and skidding into the empty throne room.

"Who let them in?" King Daniel shouted, glaring around the dais with an expression that was somehow angry and empty all at once.

A tall counselor stepped forward. "They will leave now."

"No I won't. And if anyone touches me, then I'll tell everyone what is going on here."

The King stamped a foot. "And what is that?"

Suddenly, Bart felt a funny pull. At their heart, their throat, their very being. And they weren't going to stand here and figure out which of all the crap these people were holding was the magic. Bart wasn't a mage, after all. They were just a simple damn folk.

"King Daniel, one of these here counselors is using dark magic on you to control your mind. Someone got you to stop the allotments, and I'll bet they were diverted elsewhere, for some noble cause, or so they said."

Daniel twitched. The pull on Bart grew stronger.

"Stop it!" Bart howled. Images flashed in their mind, snippets. And they stared at the King, ignoring the people to his side. "People say you are a good person. That you care. Do you feel the dark magic? Does something seem wrong?"

Wen tapped Bart's arm. They had no idea whether he'd trailed behind, or caught up. But as Bart took a breath, Wen stepped forward and his voice quivered. "My mom said you were kind, but someone has stopped the allotments. And people are hurting now, the very people who needed help the most. And they are going to have to start selling their special things, little treasures, just for food. For sleep."

Daniel blinked.

"We need you," Wen implored.

The King rose, bewilderment in his eyes, then snapped to his side. "It's you," he said, rushing toward a figure, whose shape seemed to shift, and flash. Suddenly, Daniel held a gleaming rod, as ominous as in any of MageBoss' stories, which radiated with emptiness. That was as best as Bart could say it, anyway.

The rod crumbled in Daniel's hands, and suddenly the

figure was not there. Had to be somewhere, Bart presumed, but not there.

The King turned to the other side, to a stout folk holding a tablet and dried fern quill. "Restart the allotments, 20% higher. Search any other changes made in recent sessions. Assess them. Report daily."

"Yes, Sire," the others said as they rushed back into the side hallways.

Bart sighed. They couldn't figure anything out these days. "Is this a real place or a Fantasy Land? See, I've been feeling a bit sad lately, and if you can do something nice it might take the edge off, even for a few minutes."

"Here, come on outside. And call me Danny." Danny rushed outside, and out into a courtyard filled with blossom-dotted hedges. A faint smell of something really pretty—Bart wasn't best with flowers—greeted them. Bart breathed in, then slowly out.

In the middle of the courtyard was a huge, yellow dragon, surrounded by baby dragons who were hopping and playing, bouncing little magic bubbles into the air.

On top of a small hill, swaying musicians played lively cello music, and townsfolk spun and danced around, as little secular angels tossed down biodegradable confetti which swirled into little colorful patterns and didn't get in anyone's eyes or anything.

A line of wizards stood, not just humans, but a lot of fantasy species, each carrying some pretty fancy looking wands and staffs and circlets and things, and their wizard robes had lots of embroidery, and some of them had epic type beards, even with stuff woven into them, and they all seemed to be cheerfully conferring and no one was destroying the world, just talking about making it better.

Birds chirped and flew in patterns, and squirrels sat around a picnic table playing cards and eating vegan-certified wasabi peas, and the sun peeked through huge, grand trees, and made little patterns of leaves and needles across the soft, mossy ground and over the worn pathways.

A short, handsome blacksmith with a kind smile moseyed on over with a wrought band, smooth on the inside but with dashing twists of metal around it. But it was too tall for Bart's neck and too large for a cuff. "I made this for Horse; I heard she liked fine metal work." As Horse huffed in delight, the blacksmith opened a little hinge, and clasped the thing gently around Horse's upper leg, where it sat comfortably, maybe like it was enchanted. The blacksmith nodded to Tom, who smiled back.

Looking down, Bart saw Wen, beaming and clapping. To the side, Horse flung her hair from one side to the other, her lanyards and jewels and medals and bells clinking in the sunlight and her new cuff radiating bronzed light, and three sprites circling her. Tom floated nearby, just a nice, happy friend. Old was quiet, but it looked content, and Bart patted its side.

Something felt different, but they weren't quite ready to face it. They sat back onto a bench with Old, and watched the dragon babies playing.

Just Bart: Episode 21

Cats and Squirrels

"Just trying to earn that coin . . ."

"Alright, posse. I know it's been an odd time, but the bills and the debt aren't having any of this messin' around. Time to get serious."

Tom glowed up and nodded, ghost-nodding, however that worked. Old was floating out in front, but didn't seem too involved in Bart's conversation, which apparently they were having with themself. Horse kept tromping ahead, but of course Bart couldn't avoid the fact that there were now *three* sprites dancing around her, mid-air. Happy as always. That was one thing about the sprites. Their ambiguous reality made Bart a little itchy, but the darn things sure always were happy.

Bart didn't know how to get the new sprite's attention, and they were always a bit awkward with such things. So they tried moseyin' in a side path. "Hey there, Twinkle. Sparkle," they added. Oh, maybe they shouldn't have said two names. Anyway.

All three sprites turned around, still moving along. That made Bart a bit nervous, but there wasn't really anything for them to bump into on this here stretch of open road. So they went on with it.

"Howdy. I'm Bart." They tipped their hat at the new

sprite. "They/them." Hopefully the intent here would be apparent. Thankfully, it was.

"Hi, Bart! I'm Shimmer, they/she!"

Now Bart liked the sound of that a lot. Was one thing to be respected, but another to be understood. Realizing they'd broke into a grin, Bart accidentally smiled larger. It had been so long since they'd smiled, it felt quite catching.

"Welcome. This is my posse. I s'pose you know Horse, but also this is Tom and Old. Tom's a ghost. And Old's a whiskey bottle. An antique, I think. I'm, well, I'm just Bart."

Shimmer wiggled their wings. "Hey, dude!"

Bart smiled more. Folk oughta be careful with their terms, but this sprite sure had them pegged. "Howdy, pardner," they replied, chuckling along with the sprite.

Horse kept marching ahead, but she didn't seem upset. Bart had a pretty good sense of that horse by now, for all they'd been through.

"Well, anyway, there's a town up ahead, and I haven't passed through there in a bit. As long as I can find some solid work and still keep a little distance until—"

"I've got something better," Shimmer interrupted. "No distance required. But you have to be ... *up* to it." They wriggled as if nervous. "It's a lot."

"They'll be fine," Sparkle said. Twinkle spun around in agreement, glitter flying from her sides.

All three sprites flew over toward Horse's ear, whispering. Horse stopped in place, but instead of one of Horse's portals opening up, the whole world swirled and warped around them, until they heard a soft little *pop*.

The sprites were no longer there. Horse shook her head, her various jewelry jingling with a little edge to it. She tilted her head toward Bart, then walked off to a side pasture.

"She's fine," Tom said. "We're in the small mammal multiverse. Out of respect, Horse will stay in the large mammal waiting area."

"What?" Bart paused. By this point, they really needed to stop being surprised by things, and just learn to get along. "Alright, small mammals. What about you and Old?" They didn't bother to ask about the sprites; they'd all seemed fine with whatever was about to happen.

"They don't care at all about me. And Old isn't relevant."

"Alll ... right." Bart scratched their head. "What about me? Don't think I qualify as small?" Sure, they weren't the tallest of folk and didn't like hearing conceptions about it, but humans had to at least be middling on the mammal scale.

"Sure, but what good would you be waiting in the lobby if they invited you in for a job?"

"A job," Bart repeated. Well, that's right, they'd been asking for work. "So how does this work? There's usually a town hall, right? Line up with other humans, see what's up today? Something along those lines?"

"No, you need to find The Queen." Tom glanced around. "Problem is, you won't know where she is."

"Find The Queen, but we don't know where she is," Bart repeated.

A little brown square popped into Tom's hand. 'Cept, Tom was a transparent ghost and didn't have hands so it sorta looked like they'd missed a turd. Bart kept that to themself.

"Go on, take it."

With a breath, Bart plucked the small object into their hand.

"Now just walk around."

Around? Where was around anyway? Like some sorta fairy tale, a whole landscape materialized in Bart's view. Hills, benches, ponds, swaying reeds of grass. It was right pleasant. They stepped forward, all at once greeted by a whole firebundle of chitters, chatters, rumbles, and ... meows.

A scruffy black cat, alert and with bright yellow eyes, stretched, taking their time, before slowly approaching Bart.

"I am The Queen," she said. Bart would go with she, they didn't get any read this was an ironic use of the term.

"Howdy." Bart tipped their hat. "I'm Bart. They/them." They tapped their metal pin. They weren't used to telling cats their pronouns, but this one was speaking human language, so best to be safe.

The Queen continued to stare up at Bart's hand. *Oh.* They dropped the little brown object on the ground and The Queen chomped it down. She walked over to lap some water from a fountain. Bart waited.

Bart wasn't sure whether they were supposed to ask questions, or what kind of protocol this place had, but fortunately Tom was up in their ear. Ok, Bart jumped a little, not realizing the ghost was so close.

"They can't hear me either," he said. "Well, they probably could but they don't care. So, anyway, small mammal multiverse. This is where small mammals go when they sleep."

Bart looked around. Seemed pretty nice here. *Not sure why they go back to Earth with all this going on*, they thought.

Tom seemed to hear it. "Ancient treaties. Gets complicated. Oh, here she comes." Tom poofed away.

The Queen stopped to vigorously lick her back, then turned her head forward. "You are here to perform the work?"

Bart learned a long time ago not to commit to a job without terms. "I'm here to offer my services, seein' if the work is appropriate to my skills. Also, I generally ask a fee for my services."

A loud clatter erupted around them.

"We pay professional wages for all work!" The Queen's hair rose in a few spots. "Do you think we are humans?"

Bart's face scrunched up. They weren't here to fight with a cat, but the speciesism was not necessary. Bart had enough of that dealing with some of those robots.

"And one other condition—" The Queen sat up. "No asking for Pouty P. Puss."

"I'm, I'm . . ." Bart musta looked real confused.

"One of us. He's demeaned onto Human YouTube. Prefers to be left alone here. Anonymous." Satisfied, The Queen continued on, her tone suddenly changing. "Great. First, our litter boxes are in disrepair. Snuggles, can you show them to the work?"

Snuggles seemed a nice enough cat and even let Bart pet him a while. On top of that, the place had a whole woodshop, that appeared just because Bart thought about it. So they weren't even too upset cleaning out the sandy compartments—which were all kept clean and raked—around whatever ... village this was, and framing them up nice with new wood and sturdy construction that ought to last a long while.

All sorts of folk lived here, turned out. Otters swam in the rivers, and neatly striped chipmunks sat proudly on surrounding rocks. They even saw a possum and what they thought was a hedgehog, but they kept a respectful distance.

"Mauu."

The Queen was circling around their legs, rubbing up against their britches. Bart crouched down. "Your Majesty, what can I do?"

"I'd like a palace," she said. And she stayed and talked Bart through it. Platforms and ramps, and strings hanging with bells and fluff. The project kept getting more complicated with more ideas added, but with a power drill and a staple gun and some vegan-certified wood glue, it all went pretty fast. The Queen raced up to the top platform and peered out. After licking one of her front legs, she gazed into Bart's eyes.

"This is satisfactory, Bart. Yet another task remains." Everyone grew quiet.

"Squirrel picnic tables." From around, Bart could see dozens of squirrels running across branches, and bounding between trees.

"Pardon?" Times sure were a changing and it felt like Bart couldn't keep up.

"Yes! Squirrels eat nuts. Squirrels are fancy. So why

shouldn't they dine in style? You just make a small picnic table, attach it to a fence, and alas—dining is open. No contact!"

Bart wasn't sure squirrels were the fancy ones with a cat calling herself queen and saying alas, but they were right intrigued by the idea.

Soon after, they'd crafted a whole set of small picnic tables. Turned out the construction was the same as any picnic table, but without all the walking around. They kept some natural, stained some different shades, they even got out their old woodburner, and fella, that felt good after all these years.

Bart leaned back, stretching, with their hands on their hips. A few of the animals jumped as they let out a big groan. "Sorry." They tipped their hat. "Useta' groaning with stretches."

"Humans are curious creatures indeed," The Queen stated, bounding back up to the top of the er, palace.

Looking around, Bart noticed there weren't any dogs. Sure, dogs could be large, but it was hard to forget the time the VP's wife carried a tiny dog in a bag. Bart couldn't sew worth a darn, so hopefully they didn't need any dog bags or anything. Besides . . . well, anyway.

Tom, appearing next to them, shook his ghosty head. "Nah. The Creator isn't into them. Tries not to talk about it. You know. *Touchy subject.*"

Bart shrugged. "Well, Your Majesty, any more work that I can do?"

"We are reasonably satisfied. The sun is getting low, and it will be time for me to return soon."

A whole lot of tones sounded at once, like someone ran their hands across the chimes on their drum set even though you're supposed to ask first, and then a small satchel appeared, floating in the air. Bart reached out and picked it up, finding it was heavy. Whatever coins were in there, it was plenty for the work. Bart nodded in thanks, and tied the bag to their belt for now.

"Also, we have a gift for Horse."

When it came to folk knowing about Horse, Bart no longer even asked. A large rat ran forward, with something in their mouth. Offering thanks, Bart reached for it. They went to thank The Queen, but it seemed she'd run off. Bart glanced around.

The animals all around them were returning to their activities, as if Bart wasn't even there. They stood, watching a moment, happy to see the happiness around them. Bounding, leaping, almost a song in the air. Feeling the nice heat from the sun as it lowered in the sky. But then they were . . . still standing there.

"Tom," they whispered, not trying to move their mouth too much. Bart wouldn't make a good ventriloquist, it seemed, as about half the animals turned to watch. "Tom. How do you . . . get out of here?"

"You're supposed to wake up."

They met eyes, and walked back over to find Horse. Horse was already looking their way, running her hooves against the dirt. The little cloth skirts on each hoof caught the golden light as the fringe shimmied. Bart remembered one had a fairy door on it. *Prince.* They'd forgot about that.

"Hey, Horse, The Queen gave you something." Bart held up a string, with a sequence of little metal chimes on the end, that clinked together as the string moved. "It's a cat toy, though, so I'm not sure how it—"

The cat toy blinked out of Bart's hand and was suddenly gone. "She'll play with it later," Old explained.

They weren't going to ask.

It had been a tough time lately, but something about scratching a cat's neck, and helping her with stuff, and building squirrel picnic tables had things looking up. "But we're not sure how to get out of here."

Horse huffed a bit, but with a flick of her head, a steppin-through size portal opened up right before them all. Bart sighed in relief. "Thanks, Horse, you're—"

Just then, someone stepped through Horse's portal. Onto their side.

"Bart! We're so glad to have found you. Just in time!"

Perhaps they should clarify. It wasn't just *someone* that stepped through the portal. It was someone bright yellow, with very glittery hair—though shorter than before and a bit uneven—and a big smile across his long neck. Because that's where he smiled.

"Howdy, George." Bart tipped their hat.

EarthCon Returns

"It's all somewhere else anyway . . ."

Sure enough, it was George, the same folk who'd brought them last time into EarthCon. Bart wasn't so *sure* about that there EarthCon. It had definitely been problematic before. They squinted.

"Now, how long ago was the last one?" Had it been that long? So hard to keep track.

"It runs on universal time, Bart. Hard for Earthlings to understand. But yes, it was supposed to be earlier. We delayed it in solidarity to your situation, but we're just going to say it's alright now. Don't worry; we have scanners."

As Bart started to protest, Old floated over, its marker face pensive. "It works both as escape and as satire, and I think it's about time to wrap this up anyway. Change is in the air, Bart. I say we go with it."

Bart stopped a moment, glancing between Old and George, and two seconds away from Billy Porter's Hatting out of this whole world, until they remembered they were still stuck in cat land. Rodent land. Wherever they'd gone.

George tapped his fins. "Come on, we need to go through. I was relieved to see your horse portal because no one seems to know where you've been, but *everybeing* gets nervous about using these. You can certainly understand. Here, first . . . may I?" George held out a Trek type wand.

Bart grunted or something and George took it as consent, as he scanned Bart up and down with a blue light. "All clear!"

Well, it was better than that swab, they supposed.

As they stepped through the portal, I mean, Bart couldn't really stay in the cat place, Bart spoke up. "If you've got fancy scanners and probably cures too, couldn't you give them to Earth? End the whole thing now?"

"Ancient treaties, Bart," George replied aloofly as he glanced back and forth. He seemed to relax, you never knew with galactic sorts what was actually relaxing, but Bart had a sense for it. "I've got you pre-registered; your badges should all work."

Instantly, Old's little badge appeared over its torn label. Horse's lanyard lit up and played a tiny tune. Horse gave them a knowing look, like don't worry, she wouldn't turn on the voice again. The three sprites appeared next to her, and Tom glowed up to the other side.

"I think I tossed the badge," Bart said. "Thought it was a one-year thing, and I've been living out of this bag." Thing had needed a cleaning, and Bart had swiped hard on it. "But, look, I haven't agreed to do this again. Last time, I didn't even answer any questions." Beside them, Tom snorted.

George stopped in place. Where he'd looked about to lecture Bart about their badge, his expression shifted. "Come with me, we'll get you a new badge right away. And I'll make sure the sensitivity board is aware of your concerns. Also, we are paying in Earth currency this time. Con credits in addition to—"

Bart listened intently. That wasn't as much money as they ought to feel thrilled about, but with the weird-ass random jobs Bart had been taking from robots and horses and cats and that time with the . . . *shed* . . . Bart knew their standards were low. It was coin.

With that amount of money, Bart could stay comfy a week or two and even donate to some important charities to help other folk. Change was in the air, like Old had said. Alright then. EarthCon it was. Long as it didn't get inappropriate. *Too* inappropriate.

"Alright." They tried to sound firm. "This time, I have some terms. Please tell your sensitivity board that I'd like some say in my panels: I'm not going on a vague panel about being human this time. An' they can't only be about weird westerns or simple folk, no panels about pronouns, and if it's about Earth, please make sure there's at least one other panelist from Earth. Oh. Please make my panels stuff I know about. I bet you have a database," they muttered. "And this time, I should talk some. I mean, if I take the trouble to be there."

"Of course, Bart, of course," George said, not arguing about the database. "I'll need to dilate a pinch of time to accommodate but—" A beep sounded in George's ear and he stopped and listened. "As I was saying, Bart, we're happy to help."

In an instant, light that felt too bright to be light flashed all around them. It was weird and Bart tried not to think about it. If this was some black hole thing and they came back to find Angel was 155 and hanging on in cryo to say goodbye … Well, anyway. Forget Angel. Forget software. Forget everybody.

"I don't know anymore," Tom said, hard to see in the bright lights of the hallway.

What? Bart glanced over.

"All taken care of." George inspected Bart's face but didn't seem to notice the hovering ghost. "No, don't worry. I added a reversion protocol. You'll never know the difference." Bart looked down and an EarthCon badge hung around their neck. *Ooh,* a velvet lanyard. They glanced at Horse, who Bart suspected had some role in that upgrade. Well, that was fine. Horse knew Bart liked to be comfortable, even if she was the fancy one.

Pretty soon they were all wandering down the hallways that led to other hallways. There were hand sanitizer stations all around, marked with different colors and flavors, and looking like they took credits. Bart hoped they weren't eating sanitizer, *Holy Yoko.* But if they could warp time to fill panels, they could figure all that out.

"So, I have to check on a few other guests," George was saying, glancing at his arm screen. "Your schedule and map are on the other side of the badge." One of his appendages made a flipping gesture. "Do you need anything else?"

"No, I'm sure we'll be fine. Thanks, George. And, thanks to Oprah and anyone else who helped out." George grimaced, but then he bobbed a bit before bounding off.

Shimmer hovered over. "Ops and Programming had a

huge thing over app permissions. Don't worry, I'll tell Oprah for ya."

"Thanks, Shimmer."

Bart did not need drama, so they let the topic drop, instead gazing around at the brightly lit hall, filled with excited beings of all colors, shapes, and sizes. Many glanced at Bart, but at least they were respectful and didn't approach unwanted. Maybe there were codes against that here. One point EarthCon.

Anyway, since they were in, they wound around to one of the bar stands and filled Old up with a good Michigan whiskey, using badge credits. That perked the bottle up a bit. Sitting down on a stool, they checked out their schedule.

And ... they had forgotten to ask for breaks in between panels, it seemed. There were three, back-to-back. "How's a folk supposed to get around?"

The bartender floated over and offered them three mini-ports for 3500 credits each. "Sure," Bart said, with a nod. E also gave them small bowls of pretzels, which was a nice add.

"Alright, the first one is 'Earth Buildings, Ups and Downs. Explore the vast world of Earth buildings during this exciting and dynamic discussion.'"

Bart took a drink.

Horse looked sympathetic.

"That could be anything!" Bart grumbled. "Buildings?"

Fine, though. They could spark some interest about buildings. They'd just need to steer the topic to wood framing. That was something Bart could do just fine. Look, they really shouldn't complain. As long as they didn't get relationships or family dynamics or automated test protocols or something Bart was not in the mood for—

"'Drum set basics.'" Bart did not even need to read more. Now, Bart was a bit rusty, with their set back on Grassley, but maybe the folk here wouldn't know that. They read on. "'How do you play a whole set of drums with two arms, anyway? Earthlings demonstrate the basics.'" They took a drink.

"So that will be fun, right, Bart?" Old said.

"Sure, we'll do some steering on these," Bart replied. They stared at the third panel a bit.

"'Zelda Super Fans!'" They paused, and Horse let a little whinny. "So I guess that was in their database." See that was the problem with *too* much data and not any context. "'Best moments and biggest fails, from eight bit to . . . holosuit?' I do not qualify for any of this."

"I wouldn't worry about it." Tom slid by, hovering over the bar. "Bad news is, they just violated timeline protocol full-up Biff style. Don't know what money's in that but you could make some retweetably prophetic Reddit posts. Good news is, on a fandom panel where you're not famous, you can just turn all the questions to the audience and let them talk. It'll be over before you had a chance to give'm your handle."

Bart crunched down a few more pretzels. They realized the bartender had been a bit clever selling them *three* mini-ports when they only needed *two*, but Old had its magic and Bart had panels to do, so they stood and moseyed on with the posse until they found the first panel room.

Horse asked for a souvenir EarthCon bag, so they stopped at a concession booth. The bag, made of soft fabric and printed with an image of the performer Peppermint posing in a luxe gold gown, hung nicely over Horse's side. Bart noticed that her cat toy from the multiverse had suddenly appeared inside it, along with a huge bag of something labeled **French Chips**.

A surprising number of folk were gathered outside. Apparently enthusiasm for buildings was strong in the galaxy. Surely they had buildings? Here, there were hallways leading to hallways and sometimes escalators leading to more of those, and outlooks overlooking escalators. This got Bart thinking about gravity and all sorts of things and where was it this event was actually being held, and by the time the doors opened, they almost forgot to go up to the table up front.

Now, George had said there'd be other panelists from Earth, so they looked over to see who was there. They saw . . . a beaver. As in, a beaver, wearing some sort of translation device. Next to her, well she had pronouns on her badge, was someone that Bart could recognize as an academic in any galaxy. Hey, there was a look. Not from Earth, not unless zhe'd traveled from the future, but probably someone who taught 'Earth Studies' on some distant world. Zhe was about five times Bart's height, looped over a few times, glossy violet in color, and where to look was confusing, but zhe spoke first. "Name Unable to Translate, Call Me Hruenwquihaburtrnapremme, Professor of Class M Studies University of Unable to Translate. Hello, I'm currently teaching Class M Construction at Best University: Trends and Physics."

The beaver went next. "Hello. I'm alive. I build good dams on Earth. Thanks for having me."

Bart grimaced. They'd almost said 'Hi, I'm a human' but they didn't want to sound speciesist and it seemed like a nice group. "I'm Bart. They/them." They tapped their pin, though it was on their badge. "I'm a simple folk. I've done some woodworking in my day."

"Are you a day old?" a voice spoke up from the back. The stout, globular being was wearing a Taj Mahal hat. Bart squinted. That whole hat was stoned up with rhinestones. Bart hoped they were rhinestones. Otherwise they needed to be payin' Bart more.

A magenta cloud rose up in front of the table. "You must be called on!"

The room grew silent, until the cloud finally called on the Taj hat folk.

"Are you a day old? Are you a huge baby?"

"Uh, no," Bart answered. "It's an Earth expression."

Everyone laughed politely, and a few beings took notes.

All in all, it didn't go poorly. The beaver talked about needing good logs to make a dam and wiggling them in real tight. Bart talked about how they'd always wanted to build a tower room overlooking either a forest or a city view, wherever they were living, but they never had any coin to do it. And the Professor seemed to explain why humans resisted utilizing rooftop spaces; Bart admitted they zoned out a little. This is why they'd never made it far with classroom learning. Tended to zone.

Bart felt a little embarrassed that they'd only bought one mini-port to get to each session, but they tried gathering everyone close enough and thinking together like most of the magic books they'd read, and it worked, sending them to the panel on drum sets.

That was awesome.

This panel was made of all people. There was a real nice folk from Nigeria who said he'd been to the last ten EarthCons, and he said he'd talk to Programming about the two-arm description. And then there was a disabled drummer from Finland who got the audience to turn off all their visual sensors for a while, which was a thing some of the species had never done before, and instead allow each instrument to possess its own space, as they put it. And all three of them played different sets together and demonstrated their own styles to the audience. Bart wished that panel could have lasted longer.

Bart was so excited after that one, they even signed someone's shirt with a silver pen—seemed like some sort of magic since it signed in thick glitter. The shirt was black with torn up edges and said ¡MOZART! in something sort of like a hard metal font. And now, they supposed it said MOZART – Bart, EarthCon 2020 with a scribble that was supposed to be Bart's drum set but rather looked like one of those Muppets from the rock band. Bart hoped that wasn't offensive, or licensed or anything. Bart should have just done the signature.

But they ported again, this time to the Zelda fandom panel.

Bart managed to dodge the "which was your favorite Zelda" question by instead telling a story from when they were a kid, mostly the other panelists and audience were happy to take up the time like Tom had suggested, and one of the other panelists handed out **It's Dangerous to Go Alone** bookmarks, and bookmarks always came in handy, so Bart slid that into their messenger bag.

As they walked out, they realized they hadn't agreed on where to meet up with George to get their payment. Then two humans passed, one wearing a hoodie with Japanese lettering, and one in a wheelchair holding what looked like an award.

"Join us for BarCon?"

"What's that?" Another Con, already? Maybe it was about Earth bars, or a celebration of bars around the galaxy? Bart hadn't been around lots of folk in so long, they were really just looking forward to getting back to Earth. But maybe this one paid too?

"It's where everything happens! Come on, we'd love to get to know you." The person pushed hir wheels, rolling back and then forward again.

Horse whinnied, as if interested, and Tom glowed up a little brighter.

"Well, alright then. Which way to BarCon?"

Just Bart: Episode 23

BarCon

"They said this was the real Con . . ."

It's not that Bart was particular about bars, but this sure looked like a hotel check-in area or something. A big cardboard sign surrounded by green tube lighting said **Ye Earthly Taverns** and showed a picture of what Bart was pretty sure was a screencap of Ten Forward, not anything from Earth. Well, heck, maybe Ten Forward was from Earth.

The genre thing really broke down the more one thought about it.

Anyway, Bart *was* particular about bars. Being a little snooty about something wasn't the worst, and if Bart was going to pay five times the cost for a drink, they wanted to be surrounded by comfy benches, gentle lighting, dark, lacquered wood, and a feeling that someone in the damn room gave a shit you were there.

That said, one notable thing about an extraterrestrial Con was that back on Earth, folk had sometimes glanced askance at Horse walking into their buildings, but here the whole posse just looked like they could be anyone.

Bart, their worn hat, comfortable pants, flannel shirt, and trusty pronoun pin— Horse, decked out in glitter and color and surrounded by three magic sprites of ambiguous personhood— Tom, glowing in softer tones than Bart remembered, their expression feeling far away— And Old. Dear old Old. With its magic marker face and torn label. It floated beside Bart as if it were looking for something too.

Turning, Bart almost walked into a green sort. Not meaning, froggy metaphor green, but more actual froggy green. Tall folk, wearing a **she/zhe** badge with long, wiggling arms, if you'd call them that. "Howdy. And pardon." Bart tipped their hat, wanting to step out of the being's way but realizing there was a chair blocking them.

"Yo, yo!" the being said. "Do you like my cosplay?"

Bart always cared about folks' cosplay, but this getup was slightly unclear. Plus, you never knew if someone was breaking timeline rules and dressed as some 30th century dictator or something. *Hell!* Bart hoped they didn't have dictators then. Probably would, but hopefully kept outta power. Like, they'd dictate over their minis or whatever.

Anyway, this was complicated. Bart didn't want to insult what might be part of the being's body or religious garb or something. White pants, that was brave. There was a ruffle around her neck. Oh, Bart hoped this wasn't Prince. *No, no,* they reminded themself. All admiration of Prince should be respected, however it paled. Still, they fumbled a bit, not wanting to offend.

"Napoleon!" she blurted out, spinning around.

"Oh, hey, that's great."

She wiggled in what Bart took as excitement. "Did you do EarthSim? They flew us right over Five Three City."

"No, I didn't get there. But I live on Earth."

"What?" Her arms wiggled more wiggly. "You're real? Here, want to join us? Some of my friends are industry!"

Bart wasn't totally sure what that meant.

Horse tilted her head, like "eh, she seems alright", and Tom was still staring off, but Old knew the most about this sort of thing, so they gave it the look.

"Better to talk to someone than be standing here wobbling around. I say we go."

Bart was at least glad they were sitting at the tall counter. (They'd call it a bar, but the *particular* part still held.) Normally, they liked keeping their feet on the floor, but at one of the tables they'd be staring right at someone, and that could be a lot.

A few different folk joined them. To their right, one waggled a limb. "I know, no shaking hands anymore. Isn't it funny how that just stopped?"

Bart grimaced. They'd never liked hand shaking when a firm nod would have done, but there was pain to that other folk couldn't understand.

"I'm Gvvvoooooo, many genders, any pronoun," he introduced.

"Nice to meet you." Bart nodded. "I'm Bart. They/them." They tapped their pin.

"Bart! From Earth!" This was the folk next to Gvvvoooooo now. "I'm Norto! You've met Gvvvoooooo? We're both award-winning Earthists. Always great to meet a real one, though. Earth inclusion is so important."

Bart took a drink.

Norto waved a part. "Gvvvoooooo's amazing, I got to tell you."

Gvvvoooooo laughed. "Norto is not that bad either. We make a real team, don't we?"

Bart glanced around, but the Napoleon folk, on their left, was deep in conversation with someone who looked like a large sea plant. No disrespect, and they wouldn't say that anywhere, just explaining it here in thought.

"So Bart, you're familiar with Norto's work?" Gvvvoooooo asked, before turning to the bartender. "A round of margaritos, homie!"

Bart held their own glass halfway, then set it down. "No, I'm sorry. You are … writers?"

They both stared at them a long moment.

"McDonalds, yeah, we are. We write holos. Ohh …" Gvvvoooooo paused. "You live on Earth, now? So you don't get holos?"

"I got All Access for Picard," they said, feeling less comfortable by the moment.

"If you're looking for connections, you're in the right place."

"I …" Bart was always looking for connections. Real connections. Friends. Common loves, common joys. This didn't feel like that. "I didn't really *ask* to be here. George keeps finding me. I guess he's on Programming?"

Gvvvoooooo's eye lit up. "Programming?" He glanced at Norto.

Norto leaned in. "If you've got an in with Programming,

I've had some ideas for cross-listed holo events I've been bouncing around."

Just then, a glittery folk walked up, shaped like a human, but . . . glittery. Her badge said **Candy (she/her)**. She threw an arm up over both Gvvvoooooo and Norto's shoulder area.

"Heeeey there. Just seeing if you two were doing alright."

"Bart is from actual Earth," Norto said, facial ridges rising.

"Oooooh . . ." Candy straightened up. "That's awesome!"

Now this was irritating. See, Bart had a boss that always did that; would have someone "check in" if they thought someone not important enough was talking to him. Bart could see that a mile away. Look, it was good to have a posse for trouble, but Bart did not like being "managed".

"Let me guess . . ." Candy stared at them. "Texas."

"Now that's a dang stereotype," Bart almost blurted out. At least go Dodge City with it. But this wasn't their world and frankly that was an excellent thought right now. They finished their whiskey and set it down.

"Where's that round for everyone?" Gvvvoooooo waved at the bartender. "Vier margaritos? One for the Earthling! It's on me," he added, to Bart.

"Actually, no thanks, Gvvvoooooo."

Gvvvoooooo paused a second, but Norto had leaned in again. "You know what we need to talk to Bart about? Karate baseball. I bet they'd have all sorts of ideas for it."

"Oh! Sweet Pacific!" Gvvvoooooo perked up. "K-loo just called when I was in the restroom letting me know what e was working. If I would have known, I would have told em to get over here." He tapped his screen.

"Oooh!" Candy giggled. "A new Earth fusion? You didn't tell me about this. It sounds savage!"

Something under Gvvvoooooo's shirt made an excited squishing noise, and he proceeded to pitch the idea. Maybe it was supposed to be to Bart, but as no one was looking at them, they swiveled around toward the counter, with a sigh. At least there were swivels.

Still, those patterned carpet squares. Bart knew there was a reason for them, and they might be a thing you appreciated, but never one you loved.

Horse had walked off for a bit; Bart knew she'd come back to check on them. Horse could be rather protective. Bart didn't see Tom.

Old was there, sitting on the counter. One of the bar lights shone through its glass, lighting a pretty amber glow onto the shiny black bar counter.

"How're you doing on magic?" they asked.

"I'm fine," it replied. "Just can't stop looking around at everyone. You ever admire a nice bar, Bart?"

Bart had just been thinkin' about that.

"I mean, not the room, but the bottles. The shelves they sit on. When the bottles are tall and short, and stout. Some sleek, some intricate. Different colors and styles. Custom fonts." It gazed off, dreamily.

Bart hadn't heard a whiskey bottle talk about fonts before, but they supposed they hadn't ever given bottles a proper look either. It sounded ... magnificent that way.

They resolved next time to look. Not this place. The bottles were mostly in a mini-fridge.

"The beings here, Bart," the bottle continued, "are like that too. All different kinds and all different perspectives. And yet—if I asked the bartender for my favorite gin and they didn't have it, I'd feel something missing. The world is like that, Bart. The world needs you in it."

Bart started to wonder if Old had been drinking, but see Old *was* drinking. They rubbed their eyes.

"I'm just saying, we've been through a lot but maybe some things will change. Maybe that's alright."

A wide being rolled over. The being's main body, if that wasn't an offensive way to term it, rose higher, like it had an elevation switch. But the being didn't raise into a seat. "Hi, Bart? My friends were talking about you. Just wanted to say hi. I'm Hew, just Hew."

"So nice to meet you." Bart didn't introduce themself; seemed the being had heard. "So what do you do, Hew?" They winced.

"I work max roat at the screw factory. These Cons are how I unwind."

Bart wasn't sure how to approach this, and they hesitated. They had no issue with the profession, but they didn't know much about it.

Hew seemed to get it. "Aw, no, not sexin'. We make screws. You know, out of metal, for assembly. It's a lot of the same, but it's what we've gotta do."

A bartender floated over. "More whiskey?"

The whiskey had been nice, but Bart was having

thoughts and didn't need to be fuzzy. They and Old met eyes. You know, little marker eyes.

"How about a tonic," they answered. "With lime?"

"Sure thing." The bartender zapped Bart's badge and came back with a short, sparkly glass.

"Excuse me, this is awkward," Bart said, "but it's not clear if the tips are on the badges." Bart hadn't seen anyone putting down any coin.

"It's EarthCon, not Earth," the bartender joked. "Everyone is paid fair wages, no need to grovel here for a penny." Suddenly her face fell. "Oh, I am so sorry, you are from there, aren't you?"

"No, no, no worries."

With a relieved smile—Bart was going to read what happened to her vertical mouth as a smile—the bartender floated away.

Hew had rolled past, and was talking to someone else now.

Bart was still thinking about what the bartender had said. It seemed like everywhere Bart went, Bart had heard someone tell them what was wrong with their home. They hadn't really argued it. Bart knew Earth had its stuff. But they also didn't need a Con to know it was home.

And they kept thinking. They couldn't fault a folk for being upset, but they'd seen the happy too. In that Zelda panel, all those beings of different colors and shapes and—mechanisms, all joined up in pure excitement. All about something Earth had done.

It made Bart feel better thinking about it. And if Hew

didn't mind making screws all day, that was helpful to people who needed screws.

But Bart had been so unhappy. They tried not to think about that. That's all they'd been doing, was trying not to think. Tryin' to make a dollar and help folk . . .

Horse appeared back at their side. A large neon metal ring was protruding from under her nostrils.

"Artist Alley?" Bart asked. Horse nodded, the bell around her neck jingling slightly.

"What do you want, Bart?"

Bart wasn't sure where that came from. They didn't think Horse had said it through a translator, or the sprites. Didn't sound like Old or Tom.

The bartender was drying a glass. Must have been her.

"I'd like to be an artist. A wood artist. To clarify, that's wood from trees, or maybe in the future there's wood machines and trees can stay up. I'm sorry, I'm just trying to say I want to make things. I want to make things that will make people happy. I want to help other artists, who want to make things too."

"Sounds like a plan," the bartender droned out before hurrying over to a blue person waving a badge.

This gave Bart something to think about though, something that couldn't be worked from a hotel lobby.

Bart flipped their badge over. *Instructions for a portal.* Well, sure enough. Moving up and away from the lobby-bar-place, they held the badge up and read the activation code into it.

Zwwwwip.

Still in one piece, and with the others seeming to be along, Bart smiled, yearning for the muted colors and imperfect symphony of real Earth.

And Earth it sure was.

Except right in front of them—was Bart.

Just Bart: Episode 24

A Multiverse

"Damn portals . . ."

The second-Bart was not looking Bart's way. But that was definitely themself, standing across the road, which was definitely not possible because Bart was right *here*, but was definitely possible because there they both were.

"Hoooorse? Do you know what's going on?"

Twinkle fluttered her wings. "Did you read the warning on your badge?"

Bart's EarthCon badge was still in their hands.

Instructions for a portal. Activation Code.

Warning: Do not be in your head or you may split paths into a multiverse.

"What the hell is this?" Bart asked, now just feeling grumpy. "In my head?" They hadn't asked for EarthCon, they hadn't asked for any of this. They wanted to be just . . . Bart.

"Is this like Dickens? Or Star Trek? Or *It's a Wonderful Life*? No, not that one since I'm still here. I mean, if I see myself, do I twist time forever? Did I just start an ouroboros?"

"A what?" Sparkle interrupted.

"You know, Wheel of Time. Aes Sedai."

Sparkle spun in a cloud of suddenly appearing yellow

glitter. "We're Yellow Ajah," the three sprites all chimed in.

"Sure, great. I'm Blue, but after it stopped bein' gendered." Bart stared ahead. "I don't mean to be rude, but is no one else disturbed that I'm right there?"

"They're Green," Twinkle added. "Old, you White?"

"More of a Warder?" Old offered, peeking out of Bart's messenger bag.

"This is not an Ajah scenario! I am looking at myself. Old? I think I need your help."

Old popped out of the bag, its tiny marker eyes widening then turning to dots. "Oh, well, this *is* a situation. Alright, you broke into a multiverse. So it's not really another you, it's still you."

Bart scratched their head. "So I can keep flipping to the one where I live on a cliff over Lake Superior and all the bills are paid, but before I get to the everybody's shuffled up dystopian ones."

The bottle looked tired. "No, there's one you, and no one gets to flip to anything. Bart, I think you keep asking me to—"

Suddenly second-Bart turned around, scratching their temple as Angel came running their way.

"Oh, this I do not need." They stepped back. "I'm not getting back with Angel, no matter how much you all like her. We weren't—"

"Bart," Angel said to the other-Bart. "I've tried to tell you. I need you to—"

Well, I don't need any demands.

Zwwwwip.

In a flash, they were all on a busy street. Cars were zipping by, and an elderly folk had dropped a purse. Bart rushed up. "Excuse me, you dropped this."

"Oh! Thank you, young . . ."

Bart tapped their pronoun pin.

"Yes, thank you, young person. I don't know what I would have done without this."

Bart turned back, whistling a fine tune. The whole posse was glaring.

"What?"

Old floated up higher. "This is not relevant."

"It's relevant for sure. Look, that folk dropped an important object, and what would have happened if I—"

"What now? You're going to save everyone in every multiverse? You're eternal now?"

Bart tapped their badge.

Zwwwwip.

There, they'd transported again.

Except this was different. It was like that time Horse was drunk and ported them into deep space, except there was no space.

Bart just stood, not even floated. And there was nothing. They looked around. "Ok, team, what's this?"

But there was no team. No posse. No Earth. No friends. No Bart.

Frightened—and Bart usually wasn't frightened but this counted—Bart desperately shook the badge.

Zwwwwip.

Now they were on a mountain, surrounded by rolling meadows of yellow flowers, and the soft light of the sun through a muted, water-painted sky. The chill air surrounded them, but they didn't have a coat.

Neigh!

Horse was glaring harder at them, and Tom had brightened all back up again. Old jumped back into the messenger bag. Instantly, Horse was wearing a warm ... well they didn't know if it was proper to call it a scarf or a blanket, but it looked warm and was woven with elegant maroon and silver metallic threads.

"*Diana Ross*, Horse, if you could just make everything yourself the whole time, why did—"

"Bart!" Tom swung over, shifting his ghosty shape into something that looked like glowy crossed arms. "Even I know you're deflecting here."

Bart stomped a foot. "I am not deflecting, whatever the hell that's supposed to mean. I got talked into EarthCon again, I tried to go damn home and do something about something, and now I'm on some thematically ambiguous set, like shouldn't I be at the secular heavenly saloon, and I just want to ..."

It stayed too quiet. And Bart stood still, not knowing what they were going to say and not wanting to admit they were freezing their cheekbones out here.

Horse nudged the button on her EarthCon badge.

Oh no ...

"What do you want, Bart?"

Bart tried to ignore that horse stereotype human-like

voice coming out of their friend. Friend? Well, of course. Horse had been a good friend. And Tom. And Old.

And even though Bart thought about zapping on out of here, maybe that was a question worth answering first. "Horse, can you . . . at least warm it up?"

Suddenly four tall stands appeared next to them, metal frames with a dish on top, like the ones at the bar outdoor patios on a chilly fall day. Bart relaxed, and tried not to think that they looked like they were summoning a spaceship. Maybe they should try sci-fi, one of these days. Nah, they loved magic too much. They'd had plenty of developing technology. Look what that had done for them.

"Bart?" Tom's face had taken a gentle glow. "We asked what you want."

Right. The bar heaters just had them comfortable. This was a nice mountain, and Bart liked small flowers like this.

The posse was staring at them. And the answer hadn't left.

It was still right there.

"Fine. Well, at EarthCon, I was talking to some folk named Hew, and Hew got me thinking, or maybe it was Old, and anyway, lots of things are important, like making screws, and someone has to do validation, or maybe not for the shit that gets funded for votes, but I'm good at woodworking, and it makes people happy, and maybe sometimes it's better to trust yourself than people who just want to give you shit for being you."

Horse looked like she was going to say something. She

didn't. Instead she stood there, just being a horse. And Tom was just a ghost. And Old was stayin' in the bag for now.

Holy damn, they grumbled.

Bart touched their badge.

Zwwwwip.

Second-Bart was still standing there across the road, and Angel was running their way. They didn't know why they were here, why they'd want to see something that wasn't real, wasn't even their world. Were they just taunting themself? Their gut said Angel wasn't the answer. They thought Angel knew that too.

This world's Angel stopped right in front of Bart.

"Bart, I've tried to tell you. I need you to listen to me. Please?"

There was a pause. Bart could see the other Bart wasn't listening. But they didn't leave. And Angel stepped forward.

"No matter what you do, or where you go, I will always love you," she said.

Bart didn't know they looked like that when they looked at Angel. It was . . . confusing. They still didn't speak.

"Maybe you'll need that, and maybe you won't," she continued. "But there's one thing that I know you need."

Bart froze.

"You need to take care of yourself."

Second-Bart still didn't answer. They slung on their bag and kind of stormed off, and this-Bart felt sort of weird about that. Feeling real awkward, they turned to the posse. The posse said they were Bart's friends, right? Maybe a folk could be awkward around friends. The real ones. "Is there a place to go?" they asked. "A safe, reasonable place where a folk can think?"

Zwwwwip.

Bart thought maybe they'd arrive at a calm swing in a little forest. They'd always wanted one, and it'd been in their reach once. But then they'd spiraled, one thing after another, and soon nothing was left in reach.

Everyone said Bart had failed.

The place they went to wasn't a swing, and there were never enough trees. It was a game night, one from a while ago. Bart didn't want to name all the folk there, it was too hard right now to get into it.

Bart knew who they were.

They sat back and took off their hat. They ran a hand through their hair, and let out a long sigh. The *Wildflowers* album was playing, and the dice rattled across the table. Someone was laughing, and then it caught like fire, and laughter roared and crackled across the room, warming all the chill left in Bart's bones.

The things they'd lost weren't coming back.

And Bart couldn't be here anymore.

Zwwwwip.

Bart stood in the middle of a dusty street. The sunset poured golden light down onto the wood-planked roofs, and the steeple of the tall, one-room church sparkled as the rays of light played through its edges.

A tumbleweed blew across the street. Somewhere, in the distance, Bart could hear children playing. Laughing.

Not sure who was even watching, whether watching

was even a thing here, they sauntered up to the saloon. Before they got to the stairs, the door opened, and a familiar figure walked out onto the porch.

As she turned to check that the door had shut proper, her red and black skirts swirled around, the back gathered up into a carefree bustle, pinned in the shape of a huge wild rose. She turned back. Her hair was swept into a rounded coiffure, with a few golden curls framing her warmly smiling face and distinctive brown mark. She wore an off-white shirt, with loose sleeves, and a line of neat buttons and soft lace up the front, blooming into a casually standing lace collar, circling her in waves.

Bart was a simple folk, but Miss Kitty was always worth admiring.

"Heya, Bart."

Bart tipped their hat. "Miss Kitty," they offered. "I appreciate you meeting me like this."

"Anytime. You know that."

Bart hesitated. "Is this fair use? I don't think you're supposed to converse." Bart had no ethical issue with this, and pretending she was someone else didn't seem right, but they liked to do right.

Miss Kitty stepped down the wood steps, the evening dust seeming to part to let her through.

"Do you mean to tell me that you think Miss Kitty would take issue over a few lines of whimsy?"

Bart's face flushed. "No, she surely would not."

Kitty tilted her head. "Now, why are you here?"

Why was Bart here? Was it to ask about how a folk is

supposed to take care of themself when the ways they have to make money won't allow it? And without the money, they can't do it? That not everyone had time to wait for society to be kinder?

Kitty knew all that. She'd agree with Angel. She'd tell them to take care of themself anyway, to do their best.

So was that the plan? Were they here, then, asking permission for the thoughts in their head? Just like they'd said, Kitty would tell them to follow their gut.

As for everyone else, there wasn't a magic in the world that would make them understand, it seemed. And they knew what Kitty would say to that too; family is made of bonds between folk. No one got to be a folk's family unless the folk agreed.

Bart had lost some family. And they'd find more family, they knew it. Everyone had a family out there. Everyone.

"I'm worried I've wasted time," they blurted out. Bart shuffled their boot. They didn't like blurting things out, it felt . . .

"Are those pineapple leather?" Kitty nodded at Bart's boots.

That did crack a grin. "Yes, they are. I got them for helping someone."

Kitty gave one of those wise smiles that annoyed Bart a touch. Ok, sure, they'd helped some folk along the way. For sure, whenever they could. That wasn't wasted. But they couldn't keep going on, unsure, worried about coins, worried about everyone else . . .

"Bart? All those people who see another version of you,

they aren't posse. Posse are the people who help you be who you are. To do what you need to do."

Well, damn it, she *was* giving the lecture on family after all that. Maybe that was ok. Maybe Bart needed to hear it. To believe it.

She went on. "Wasted time, the whole concept of it, is a thing people who aren't posse say. It's like making a fresh tomato sandwich with a pinch of salt, then someone tells you you should've had the avocado. What good does that do? Maybe you couldn't reach the avocado, and if they wanted you to have it so much, they could have offered one then." Miss Kitty held a little fire in her eyes now, despite her calm expression. "All of this, Bart. All of it is you. You did what you did. You got through it, day by day. You're still here. So what are you going to do now?"

Bart looked around, and saw the posse standing around them.

Horse was staring back up the road, still wearing the scarf from the mountain and everything else she'd picked up along the way. Tom floated, distracted, almost hard to see in the light. Bart could feel the weight of Old, resting in their bag.

They watched Miss Kitty walk back up the steps, and into the saloon, and normally Bart would stop in for the best whiskey she'd offer them, but the sun was setting. Bart had best find themself an inn, and get some rest.

Tomorrow would be a new day.

Just Bart: Episode 25

Another Day

"Another dollar . . ."

Bart took a last look around the room. A borrowed space wasn't just borrowed for the days you were in it, it was borrowed for the memories it gave you.

The bed, a nice window, a little coffee stand. It had been nice. And if this was the end, Bart decided to make a cup of coffee first. They were glad to see the oatmilk in the mini-fridge; when this started that wasn't even a thing. Not that they'd ever abandon the hug of a smooth cashew cream with a touch of maple syrup.

They sat on the bed, and stared out of the window, finishing the coffee and just . . . sittin' a bit.

Suppose it was time.

A bag over their back, they didn't say goodbye to the folk here again. They'd done it already, and everyone knew how much they appreciated the kindness they'd been shown. Strange times were good times for kindness, Marma used to say.

In fact, Bart had always tried to be just, but a new realization of that had set in. What they really meant by it was they'd like to be *kind*. When a folk was truly kind, the justice parts found all the right places to settle.

Winding down the stairs, Bart stepped out onto the

road. It was still a dusty road, for now, with a whole bunch of tumbleweeds on it. And passersby. All of them queer, too. Bart added that. And ... parasols. And some birds. Happy birds.

And Horse was walking over, the early light reflecting real shiny on her body, at least in the places Bart could see it under everything else.

Bart tipped their hat. Horse nudged her face against theirs, and held it for a long moment. Then stepped back. Horse didn't look sad, in fact she looked content. Bart tried to take that feeling with them, too. They almost said that they'd miss her, but that didn't feel right.

"Horse, it's not just that you're cool, you've been a good friend to me, and I think we'll always be friends."

Horse let out a slightly indignant breath, and looked as if she was waiting for something.

Bart couldn't help but laugh.

"Ok, fine, and you're cool too. You, and your horse hair, and that spot on your back, and your sense o'humor, and your magic abilities, and your unbothered sprite friends, and that pretty blanket, and your hair clip, and hair ribbon, and crystal bracelet with the deft chainmaille work, and that awesome handmade nose ring, and your sparkly lanyard with sparkly wizard dice and that gaming tournament medal and metal garden bell, and your custom name necklace, and your Peppermint bag with the cat toy in it, and your tooth gem, and your leg cuff, and hoof covers and fairy door, and your ear tiara and glass charm, and that rainbow hair extension and lacy tail tutu, and that painted hair and the magic sparkle spot, and . . ." A small glint of red caught their eye. They'd forgotten the least fancy item of all: the tiny gift Angel had given her. "And that pretty red bead."

No one translated Horse this time, nor did Horse speak. Horse was just Horse, and Bart could hear her in their mind.

You're cool too, Bart. I need you to believe it more, and I really think good things will happen. But if you're having second thoughts, it's raining glitter in the multiverse. We could go check it out. After that, I'm stopping into a horse disco and visiting some old friends, just off of assignment. No rule I know against taking you along. The parties can get pretty wild, though. Get it?

Horse snorted, as though chuckling.

Bart smiled. That horse disco might be right fun, and Bart would set that thought aside for the next time they needed it. "No, Horse. Thank you, but our paths are different; I can see that now. But gettin' to know you has helped me in ways that are dug too deep to describe. I'm sure you'll be needed elsewhere, to help someone else." In fact, Bart had caught a glimpse of that, in the multiverse. Horse, with someone else. Bart wondered how old Horse was.

The red bead glinted in the light. And that gave Bart an idea. About something they'd forgotten, with everything else.

"If you're off to the horse disco, you'll want to look amazing there. And I've just got one thing that might help. You don't need help, but anyway, it's what I've got."

Horse made a gentle sound.

Bart fumbled around in the bag's side pocket, finally

pulling out a chunky silver ring. They threaded it up into Horse's mane, and tilted the red bead to let the ring barely pass overtop, where it rested nicely and looked secure.

"There. You'll be a proper Mr. T now. You know, he started out as a bouncer on Rush Street, collectin' pieces left behind."

Is this someone I should know? Please tell me he's not like Mr. Ed.

"Oh, hell no. And, yes. I mean, no. At this point it would be too confusing to explain the whole vibe. Especially now that he's on Twitter mostly talking about God."

What?

"Don't worry about it. Anyway—" Bart didn't have the right word for this moment and all it meant, so they tipped their hat. Horse nodded back. Then one of Horse's glowing portals opened, and Horse stepped through, jingling brightly. As it closed, Bart could see the three sprites, dancing in a happy circle.

Maybe Bart just couldn't handle dwelling on a moment like that, but they did immediately have a strange thought. Tom seemed like the sort that would have glowed up right away at the mention of a folk like Mr. T. Bart walked up and down the street, as queer passersby twirled their parasols, and said good day to each other, and the sun rose higher in the sky.

Bart stopped. He wasn't there anymore; Bart knew it. Or he felt ... different. There was something in Tom that Bart knew was comfortable now. And so Bart let him be.

"Guess it's just you and me now, Old."

Bart kept on down the street, and without a horse and a ghost at their side, it was a lot easier to hail a cab.

The place was nice. It wasn't fancy, and Angel had dropped off the rest of their things, from the few places they'd been gathered. That included Bart's drum set. *Sweet Prince,* they hoped the neighbors hadn't seen that going up the elevator. Maybe someday.

Angel had insisted it was neither a loan nor a gift, and just said a few people had pitched in. "It's faith," she'd called it, letting them know the first three months' rent were covered, along with utilities, if they didn't go too far with that. And on top of that, three months sharing the wood shop co-op a few blocks over, in the basement of a small contractor supply shop. And a credit toward scrap wood. Bart was most excited about that.

Seemed a cleaner had been in, and only missed a set of walnut shelves in the small studio room. Good walnut, not a stain, they noted, enthusiastic about the small surprise. Walnut wood felt like good luck. They got a cloth from the compact kitchen, and ran it over the surface of each, with just a tiny dab of water, nothing that would stay wet, until they could make a proper spray.

There wasn't too much to unpack, strictly in the literal sense, and not much for the pretty shelves then, either. There'd been a little vase of daisies left on the desk, and Bart would leave those there for now.

Bart pulled Old out of the bag. Being empty, it must be out of magic. So Bart felt a great shock when the little marker face formed on the side of the amber bottle.

"Hey, Bart. I just want you to know that I'm proud of you. And . . ."

The peering bottle looked like it had something to say.

"Can I get a hug? Look, Bart, I'm a hugger, and I know it's been a long road and maybe you're not a hugger, but." The bottle looked up expectantly.

"Get over here. Wait." Bart went back and checked that the door was locked. "Get over here." They pulled the old, weathered bottle into their arms and held it tight.

Hugs could be the nicest gifts a folk could ever get. When they were agreed to!

Looking down, the little marker face was gone.

Bart drew a slow breath, calming themself, and took the damp towel and rubbed it over Old, being extra careful around the bottle's torn label. They set it on the shelf, with a tiny tumbleweed they'd saved resting at its base.

They sat down at the worn desk by the beautiful over-painted window with the rusty hardware and a weathered, crusty screen, opening the large drawer to store their messenger bag, for now. They stopped. A shiny silver laptop sat inside, with a note on top, in Angel's scrawly handwriting. "It's from someone named Jared who saw my post. Do good with it. Or hell, do whatever."

Another drawer had some accessories, and before long, Bart was up online. Bart did not love web work, but sometimes stuff had to be done, and with things as they were, getting an online shop would be real important. They could wear a mask at the wood shop and stay away from folk, but conventions were out of view for just now. At least that experience in software would come in handy.

Setting up wasn't as bad as they'd thought. They set up listings for dice towers, mini-tables, rolling trays, and small storage boxes for now. They were meeting with MageBoss in Discord tomorrow to talk about some combo sets. Wizard-fired dice plus a polished wood case in one bundle, with the wood chosen to complement the dice. Per was finally doing better, per said.

Bart also wanted to try making little treasure chests, some sized for cards, others with a removable tray to store dice, and maybe some larger ones for tokens or meeples.

Meeples! Bart would love making little meeples. Plain for painting, or sealed up to show the nice woods. They suddenly had the idea of making the prettiest little horse meeples the world had ever seen. Not just for gaming, but for collectibles. They had a good friend in a group home who didn't have lots of shelf space. Bart could see sending em a little line of happy horses, made of all the kinds of wood they could get from the scrap.

See, these were ideas for the future. They'd need to start somewhere, and try to get an audience and hope they could make some sales.

They knew it was going to be hard, and that it would be hard again, but there was light shining in through the old window screen, and Bart had a laptop and a nice pair of boots, and a dusty trail that might lead to making some people happy. And, getting back to the shelter, maybe some cats too.

Bart needed a little more software for the banking piece, and they set up the download for the client-side. Waiting for the file to complete, they browsed around the web for a minute.

The news was sad, and stressful. People were being self-centered, and stubborn about tired, hurtful things, and Bart unfriended a few people who were making awful posts and not likely to care. That made them sad.

Sometimes feeling sad led to someone feeling sadder, and Bart felt scared, alone in a small room, without a posse. Just Bart.

Could they do this?

Ba-ding.

A little message popped up in the corner of the screen.

Bart! Haven't seen you for a while. Wanted to check how you were doing. I heard you were looking to run a game supply shop. That's awesome! I know you can do it, and I'll do my best to spread the word. Don't give up. Sometimes it takes a while, and we're here for you. Anyway, hope you're well and hoping we can get together when it's safe.

Bart stared at the screen, and feeling a smile spread across their face, they started to type.

They had a posse.

They have you.

JUST BART: THE END

Mosey on by:
edebell.com

www.ingramcontent.com/pod-product-compliance
Lightning Source LLC
Chambersburg PA
CBHW021123190726
48288CB00008B/2468